Russ Pinkerton

S0-BBH-608

Love's Destiny

ARLENE COOK

HARVEST HOUSE PUBLISHERS
Eugene, Oregon 97402

Scripture quotations are from the King James Version of the Bible.

LOVE'S DESTINY

Copyright © 1985 by Harvest House Publishers
Eugene, Oregon 97402

ISBN 0-89081-470-8

All rights reserved. No portion of this book may be reproduced in any form without the written permission of the Publisher.

Printed in the United States of America.

To my sister, Phyllis.
Like Felicia, armed with faith and love,
she has set out to conquer
a new frontier for the Lord.

1

"*H*old on!" yelled the leathery old driver above the stinging crack of his whip.

The hot, dust-covered stagecoach moaned tiredly, then lurched forward, flinging the four occupants of the westward-bound stagecoach against one another and sending their lunchbasket and handcases crashing to the floor.

Twenty-year-old Felicia Maria Worthington Las Flores reached down and quickly gathered the long, full skirt of her crinolined brown-wool traveling dress close around her as Mr. Jenkins, the lone gentleman in their party, attempted to retrieve their scattered belongings.

Suddenly the portly banker choked on the swirling road dust mushrooming up through the floorboards. With the help of his fragile wife and Felicia's Aunt Winnifred, Felicia was able to raise Mr. Jenkins and push him back into his seat amid the wild sway and bounce of the speeding coach.

"What ails that fool driver?" bellowed the red-faced Jenkins.

"This rickety old contraption will break apart if he doesn't slow down!" warned his panic-stricken wife.

"If he and Shotgun Sam don't fly off into the gorge first!" cried Winnifred Worthington as the carriage leaned frighteningly far out over the edge of the ravine before righting itself. It was all the passengers could do to hang on.

The driver cracked the whip again and again, spurring the heavily-lathered team of horses along the washboarded Santa Fe Trail.

"At least at this stride," Felicia called out above the sounds of squeaking springs and thrashing wheels, "we'll leave this desert inferno behind sooner than we'd hoped."

Then Felicia added silently, *Sooner to San Diego and to my father's bedside. I must reach him, talk to him—before it's too late!*

"We can't arrive too soon for my taste. I've been looking forward to a change of scenery and temperature since the day we left New Mexico weeks ago," complained Mrs. Jenkins.

Felicia was sympathetic. "Those tree-covered foothills ahead will lift us gradually to a pass that cuts through the mountain range on the horizon. From there it's downhill all the way to the cool breezes of the Pacific Ocean and the pueblo of San Diego.''

Even though Felicia's melodic voice strained above the clatter, her tone was reassuring to the elderly couple who looked to her as somewhat of a tour guide.

Is it because I'm a teacher that they trust my knowledge of geography? Felicia mused. *Or am I an authority on cross-country travel because Aunt Winnifred and I started our journey in Boston, weeks before they came aboard in Kansas City?*

She studied the couple seated across from her. *They can't possibly know that I've traveled this treacherous territory before, or that I am a native Californio, born on Rancho El Camino.*

She turned and glanced at Aunt Winnifred sitting beside her. The intense desert heat caused the freckles dotting her aunt's cheeks and the bridge of her nose to swim together. Except for the fact that the damp, carrot-red ringlets peeking from the edge of her bonnet were streaked here and there with silver, Felicia's favorite aunt looked much like a young schoolgirl who had just finished a game of hopscotch on a hot summer's day.

She did not have the natural wasp-waist that Felicia had. Still, Aunt Winnifred's boyish figure gave her the agility and appearance of a woman much younger than her forty-five years. Although opposite in coloring, the two women had the same small frame and each stood exactly five feet two inches in stocking feet.

When they were first introduced to the Jenkinses, a question concerning the family patriarch arose. Aunt Winnifred, as always, was quick to tell the truth. She stated proudly that her brother, Felicia's father, son of English parents, was himself a

Yankee-born sea captain.

What Aunt Winnifred didn't share with their fellow passengers was that burly, red-bearded John Worthington had years before become a naturalized Mexican citizen and had commanded a Mexican brig, the *Capistrano*, off the shores of California. Then, in 1825, Worthington married Felicia's mother, the beautiful Spanish niece of a Mexican governor. Worthington left the sea after he petitioned the governor and was awarded a land grant—eleven leagues, or approximately 48,000 acres, of virgin land located north of San Diego. It was then that Captain John Worthington changed his name, as was the custom, and became Don Juan Las Flores, Don of Rancho El Camino.

Felicia tried to swallow the lump rising in her throat. It seemed to build each time she thought of the part of her proud heritage that she was forced to hide from the world "out East."

"For your own well-being, tell no one of your half-breed background while you are in my care and attending Mount Holyoke Seminary," Aunt Winnifred had insisted the moment she and her younger twin sisters arrived in Boston from California six years earlier. Aunt Winnifred's stance did not soften, even when Felicia enrolled in the more liberal Normal School to be educated as a teacher.

Felicia sighed to herself. *And that was before the war broke out between the United States and Mexico! What would my Yankee friends think of me now as battles rage in the Far West and Americans fall to Mexican bullets?*

My father, born in Boston, the son of English citizens, eventually acquired Mexican citizenship. My mother, born in Spain, later sailed to Mexico, where she became a Mexican citizen. I'm half-and-half.

Which half is what? Even if it were sorted out, would my friends remember that in my heart I'm 100 percent American?

A strong jolt brought the dark-lashed young woman back to the moment. She turned her attention out the open window, to the barrenness of the cactus-and-scrubbrush terrain surrounding their speeding coach. She gazed upward to the top of the bluffs that rose straight above the river on the far side of the ravine.

Felicia's dark Spanish eyes, set against the pure alabaster complexion she had inherited from her Castilian-born mother, drank in the beauty of the pastel-shaded layers of rock that formed the cliffside.

Felicia reached up with her delicate, slender fingers and brushed away a loose strand of thick, ebony-colored hair that had escaped from the bun at the nape of her neck. A straw bonnet protected the heavy satin sheen of her tresses from the road dust and the unrelenting sun that beat down upon them, even in late November. A dark-brown bow tied under her chin completed a frame that complemented her perfectly featured face.

It was then that her searching eyes caught a glimpse of something—a cloud of dust rolling along the top of the cliffs. Felicia's eyes narrowed. It was keeping pace with them!

"Look out my window, Aunt Winn. There... high on the bluff you'll see what our driver is running from."

The Jenkinses, as well as Miss Worthington, looked to where Felicia pointed.

"Indians!" exclaimed Jenkins.

"I thought we left worry behind when we crossed the Colorado River," wailed Mrs. Jenkins. "After all, this is 1846. We are a civilized nation!"

Civilized? scoffed Felicia silently. *Were we civilized I could boast that my mother, God rest her soul, was a darling of the Spanish court before she married my father. When my friends remark on my "exotic" looks I could say proudly that my father believes that I resemble my mother exactly.*

Felicia's eyes hardened as she watched a dozen Indian warriors race along the cliff top. *Civilized? If so, Father would not have fearfully packed up his three daughters and sent us East to be educated, visiting us only once in the last six years, when he sailed to Boston to negotiate a contract to sell hides to shoe manufacturers.*

"All because of Indian raids on the ranchos!" Felicia spat aloud.

"What did you say, Miss Worthington?" Julius Jenkins called out before his voice was drowned by a long screech and the shudder of braking wheels.

"We're going downhill toward the river," reported Mrs. Jenkins, clutching her husband's arm tightly. "Thank heaven, those wild men are stuck up on that mesa!"

"Once we ford the river we'll be heading up into the trees I mentioned," consoled Felicia, glad for a change of subject.

"Then we'll be on the Indians' side of the river!" At her own revelation, Ophelia Jenkins threw her other arm around her husband's neck and began to sob.

The stagecoach splashed into the shallow river. Felicia reached over and took her aunt's trembling hand into her own. The carriage swung from side to side as it moved cautiously across the rock-strewn river bottom. The two women did what was their custom when crisis loomed in their daily lives. They bowed their heads and prayed silently for God's protection.

Felicia knew that the Indians toying with them had to be Yuma Indians, vicious scalp-hunters who roamed freely from the Colorado River west to the San Diego back-country ranchos.

Felicia felt her anger deepen. *Indians have kept me from my father for six years. They are directly responsible for. . .*

She quickly touched her hand to her breast. Yes, the letter was still there, safely hidden—for the moment, anyway. No place would be safe if the Indians attacked.

Felicia's eyes filled with tears. She held back the sobs swelling in her chest by concentrating on the exact wording of the secret letter sent to her by her father's majordomo.

"Senorita Las Flores," he had begun in his large scrawl, "it is with sadness that I report the Don's declining health due to an Indian raid upon Rancho El Camino last week. I am writing to you without the Don's permission. Please come with haste before it is too late. Your father's faithful household prays for your safe journey home."

The letter was dated five months earlier!

Felicia brushed the tears from her sleepless eyes and looked upstream. There, coming around the bend in the middle of the river, was the band of Indians! Their naked, muscle-taut bodies glistened in the sunlight. The bright colors streaming from their war bonnets, along with the regimental formation of their spirited mounts, made them appear as festive and harmless as an Independence Day parade. But one look at their deeply lined faces, even at a distance, sent a shiver of fear racing through her body. Felicia watched, wide-eyed and speechless, as the advance guard of deadly killers moved toward them like a swelling wave.

Pray, all in Father's household! Pray!

A lightning snap of the whip and the horses pulled sluggishly forward against the brisk current. Another snap and the coach jumped. The horses' hooves pulled up on solid ground at the river's far edge.

Felicia heard the water drain from the bottom of the stage, making it lighter with each foot they traveled up the winding path through the grove of winter-naked, deciduous trees.

No advantage will help us now, she thought. *We can't even hide from them as we run.*

Felicia watched Mrs. Jenkins pull off her wedding ring and hand it to her husband, who looked perplexed as to where to secret it. Just then the coach turned the bend and the group got a quick look at the trail behind them.

"They're gaining on us!" exclaimed Aunt Winnifred frantically. "And look! Their bodies are covered with tattoos!"

Ophelia Jenkins fumbled in her crocheted handbag and pulled out her handkerchief. The pungent odor of smelling salts filled the cab. "It's no use," the woman cried, inhaling deeply.

"Don't give up!" ordered Felicia, her dark eyes flashing angrily. "Remember, nothing happens that isn't under God's control. We still have time to. . ."

Suddenly a shot rang out. Then another. Or was it the sound of the first shot reverberating through the trees?

"Now they're shooting at us!" gasped Jenkins.

"I don't think so," scowled Felicia, getting another quick glance back down the trail. "The

Indians have stopped short and are looking around.''

''Then it had to be our own Shotgun Sam firing as soon as those savages galloped within range,'' suggested Aunt Winnifred.

The coach crested the hill and started down the far side.

''An answer to prayer. We're safe from return fire for the moment.'' The relief in Jenkins's voice seemed to comfort his distraught wife.

Another report pierced the air. Closer this time. The stagecoach slowed.

Without warning Aunt Winnifred stuck her head out the window and called up to the driver. ''What's going on?'' she demanded.

Felicia's face turned ashen. She grabbed her aunt by the waist and jerked her back into the coach. ''Aunt Winnifred! Next they'll be shooting at you!''

A moment later the coach slowed, then finally came to a dead stop. Even before the dust settled, the air was alive with the sounds of male voices and clanking sabers.

''It's an ambush!'' Ophelia Jenkins slurred, just before she fainted in her husband's arms.

Felicia gripped Aunt Winnifred's arm, lest she try to poke her head out of the window once again. The coach jiggled unnervingly as the driver and Shotgun Sam climbed down from their perch.

Jenkins shoved the smelling salts under his wife's nose. She choked and slapped his hand away.

''What's your guess, Felicia?'' Winnifred Worthington asked in a low whisper. ''Could it be a posse of Californios?''

''What are Californios?'' inquired Jenkins seriously, wiping his wife's red and runny eyes with his own handkerchief.

"Revolutionaries." Aunt Winnifred replied quickly.

"Defenders of Mexican soil and..." Felicia's attempt to elaborate was cut short by the sound of voices approaching the door of the coach.

Physically and emotionally exhausted, the passengers in the cross-country stage could do no more. An expression of hopelessness crossed the faces of the couple from Kansas City. They sank back in their seats and closed their eyes, resigned that their worst fear was now an imminent reality.

My spirit is not so easily broken, thought Felicia defiantly. Unobtrusively she slipped her fingers into the thick velvet cuff at her wrist and withdrew a long hatpin. Aunt Winnifred quietly did the same.

The coach door sprang open.

There, standing against the late afternoon sun, was a tall man in his early thirties with sun-streaked blonde hair and a vertical scar that cut a swath from his left cheekbone to his square-cut jawline. He looked trail-tired and hunger-gaunt. What had once been a parade-ready captain's uniform was tattered, torn, and dirty—and hung loosely from his broad shoulders.

Felicia held her breath, cautiously assessing the handsome stranger as his eyes, the color of green ice, scanned the faces of the other passengers. Then he looked directly at her, capturing her eyes with his and holding them. She looked back at him for a long moment, meeting his searching curiosity with her own. She felt her heart begin to beat ever faster. She quickly lowered her thick, dark lashes as a light blush crept over her high cheekbones.

With her eyes still lowered, Felicia sent a prayer heavenward. *Please, Lord, not a renegade! He's too. . . handsome.*

Just then the proud officer stepped back a pace, held the door open wide, and proclaimed with a flourish, "Ladies and gentlemen, the First Dragoons of the United States Army, veterans of the frontier, welcome you to California."

With a sweeping bow he added, "Please join us for dinner."

2

*T*ears of relief filled Felicia's eyes, then brimmed over and ran joyously down her cheeks. She quickly dabbed the runaways with her mother's lace handkerchief, leaving a crystal sparkle clinging to her long lashes.

"Captain Fletcher Crane at your service, Miss ..." voiced the officer, offering Felicia his hand. She took it. His grasp was firm and self-assured.

"Worthington, Felicia Maria," she replied, deciding quickly that this was not the time or place to reveal her California heritage.

She stepped lightly to the ground and looked around uncertainly. "The Indians chasing us. . .?"

Captain Crane smiled down at her. The ice in the green of his eyes seemed to melt at the edges. "Be troubled no longer. You are now under the protection of General Kearny's forces. A contingent of men was dispatched to your aid the moment we spied your coach rounding the bend and heading down the steep grade to the river."

"Then we were never really in danger. . .?"

The Captain smiled, broadly this time, showing a row of beautiful white teeth. "Oh, most certainly you were. But fortunately, the U.S. Army was near at hand. It will not take our men long to rout those scoundrels."

Felicia looked up at him questioningly. "But they're scalp-hunting Yumas. They—" She stopped when she felt him tense.

"How would a young lady from Boston know so much about local Indians?" Crane asked sharply.

He took Felicia's arm and guided her to the side of the trail, leaving the other officers to escort the remaining passengers. The captain stopped near a clump of wild buckwheat, rested his hand on the handle of his saber, and awaited her reply.

Felicia's mind raced as the color rose in her cheeks. She was not a traitor, and she would not be treated as one! Felicia met his accusing eyes without flinching. "My father lives near San Diego. His health is failing due to injuries suffered in an Indian attack. I'm trying to reach his bedside before—"

"Please. . .I did not mean to sound insensitive."

Captain Crane rose to his full height and went on to explain.

"This is not a textbook war. The enemy does not wear a common uniform. Let's take the Indians, who are close at hand. Some California tribes are sympathetic to the Americans, having been well-treated by us for a generation. Other savage nations side with Mexico. For the most part, the natives are neutral or are out to cause trouble on their own. The Yumas are an example of the latter."

"What does all of this have to do with me?" Felicia's eyes flashed their own warning of outrage toward her interrogator.

Crane was silent a moment while he appraised her. Then he spoke, a bit warily, Felicia thought. "We hear that the Californios are somewhat the same—divided in their loyalties, whether they be of American, Spanish, or Mexican descent."

Felicia forced a demure smile. *He'll not entice me into a political discussion. Better he should think that I am incapable of carrying on an intellectual conversation than to know who I really am! If he knows anything about the Dons, he'll conclude that my father's relinquishment of his U.S. citizenship makes him a flag-waving supporter of Mexico's General Pico, leader of the Californios—leader of the enemy!*

Felicia's private musings were interrupted by a heavy sigh from the Captain. It was as if he had come to some final determination about her.

"Forgive my suspicious nature," he said, his eyes surveying hers. "I should know that only an emergency could entice a well-bred young lady, such as yourself, to travel alone cross-country through Indian territory and into an international war zone."

Felicia's response was quick. "I am not alone, Captain. My father's sister is accompanying me and. . ." Felicia started to gesture Aunt Winnifred's way when she suddenly realized that she was still carrying the lethal hatpin in her left hand. Embarrassed, Felicia felt her vexation flee. She smiled and held up the hatpin for Captain Crane to see. "You see, we were prepared for battle."

Crane chuckled, dissolving the remaining tension between them. "My dear, you do have the fighting American spirit. The First Dragoons have an abundance of that also. And we'll not quail when we encounter the enemy—who is marshaling its forces somewhere between here and San Diego."

Then the Captain's face lost its smile as he quipped, "But we're a little like you with your hatpin, trying to take on a tribe of scalp-hunters!"

"What do you mean?" she asked, as Captain Crane turned and led her to a well-concealed path through the wall-high chaparral bordering the trail.

The path opened up to a clearing which was the company encampment area. A large piece of sizzling meat hung low over an open fire. Several yards away three officers, as trail-worn as Captain Crane, were instructing men repairing a wheel on a wagon filled wtih military equipment. Two of the men were without shoes. Another officer was cleaning one of two howitzers in their arsenal. Across the clearing, other soldiers tended a pathetic accumulation of half-starved animals.

Finally Crane spoke. "The answer to your question starts with that man standing next to Captain Johnston, the one dressed in trappers' buckskins and measuring head-high to the Captain's collar bars. His name is Kit Carson. He's not a military man, although Colonel Fremont gave him the rank of lieutenant on special service."

"I don't understand. What does Mr. Carson have to do with General Kearny's march to California?"

"We set out for California from Fort Leavenworth in July to fight the Mexican Army and to end the war begun officially in May. About 700 miles east of here, along the Rio Grande River in New Mexico, we met up with Carson, who was bearing dispatches for President Polk from Commodore Stockton and Fremont, saying that the conquest of California was all but over. General Kearny ordered most of our men back to Santa Fe and 'persuaded' Carson to defy orders and lead the remaining 110 men on to California."

Felicia noticed while he was talking how dry and sunburned his skin was. It was obvious that both man and beast had suffered greatly.

"Then what happened?" she asked.

"We encountered a group of Mexicans with a large band of horses, on their way to Sonora to plead for help in the war against us. Next we captured a Sonoran in whose saddlebags were found dispatches to Mexican General Castro. The Mexican Army will be ready for us."

"And you are not at full strength . . ." Her voice faded as her eyes scanned the panorama before her. Men, many without boots, others near-naked, all of them hungry, labored wearily.

Then from somewhere beyond the perimeter of the camp came a long, lone howl—echoed soon after by the pack's response.

Felicia stiffened.

"It's all right, Miss Worthington. Those are not

your Yuma Indians. They're coyotes—camp followers, if you will, circling, waiting for us to abandon more horseflesh along the trail." Then Crane added cryptically, "They've had quite a banquet lately."

"Oh, no," Felicia uttered, picturing the soulful look in the eyes of horses and mules abandoned on the desert trail. There was some consolation. Now that the Army had reached the foothills, there would be plenty of winter grass for the remaining animals and some wild game for the men.

Lord, give them time to replenish themselves physically, emotionally, and spiritually before they encounter General Pico's forces.

Crane suddenly slipped his arm around Felicia's shoulders and pulled her close for just a moment as if to cheer her. "Don't worry," he said, "they didn't get our best horseflesh. We've saved that for our own feast tonight." He nodded toward the meat turning over the spitting flame.

Felicia felt the color drain from her face.

Later, after the driver pulled their overdriven team off the trail and into the protected encampment area, the ladies were permitted to return to the coach and gather a few personal belongings and their handcases.

A young soldier, assigned to the womenfolk for their protection, led them to a secluded spot behind an outcropping of large granite boulders.

"Look, a spring bubbling out of the rocks!" exclaimed Aunt Winnifred. "Is that pool too deep for bathing, Corporal?"

"No, Ma'am. Just a bit on the chilly side. The early snow on the mountain peaks is already running into the spring. Perhaps you'd just prefer to wash up."

"You'll never know what we'd prefer, young man," Aunt Winnifred replied with a twinkle in her eyes, "unless you decide to make camp here."

The young corporal's face turned beet red. "I just left, Ma'am." He turned on his heels and ran.

The three women giggled and immediately started shedding their heavy outer clothing. No matter how cold the water was, Felicia decided any temperature would be worth the price of total cleanliness for the first time in weeks.

While her aunt and Mrs. Jenkins bathed quickly, Felicia shook out, then beat, her dark-brown traveling suit against the rocks. It took several blows before the dust stopped flying out of the full-skirted garment.

While the other women dressed, Felicia dipped into the pond's cold water and covered herself with suds from her cherished bar of lavender-scented soap. She quickly rinsed off and dried herself with a soft hand towel. She redressed, slipping into her last clean blouse, a baby-blue cotton batiste trimmed with hand-tatted lace at the high neckline and cuffs. Her worsted traveling suit appeared fresh, once it had a chance to air.

The golden crown of the sun disappeared below the horizon just as Felicia finished brushing the hundredth brush stroke through her thick, long hair. She gathered it into a loose, youthful bun at the back of her neck and pinned it securely. She applied the tiniest amount of gloss to her lips and a tad of color to her cheeks. Finally she and the other ladies were ready to accept Captain Crane's most welcomed dinner invitation.

Conversation never lagged among the officers or their guests. Neither the war in general nor the upcoming confrontation in particular was discussed. For the officers' part, they were eager to hear of life back in Boston, a place most of them had not visited in years.

Although Captain Crane sat next to Felicia during the meal, he was careful to direct his conversation to the group as a whole. It was only after the embers burned low and he walked her to their guests' sleeping area did Fletcher Crane inquire into Felicia's personal life.

"You mentioned that your father was injured in an Indian attack. What about your mother, brothers, and sisters? I trust that the other members of your family are safe."

"Thank you for your concern, Captain. The Indian attack upon my father *is* foremost in my thoughts. My mother died seven years ago of influenza. I have younger sisters, twins, who are currently in school in Massachusetts."

"In school?"

"My father, Boston-born himself, holds the modern view that women, as well as men, should avail themselves of higher educational opportunities. In fact, both Maria and Martina plan to attend Oberlin Collegiate Institute in Ohio next term. It's one of the trailblazing colleges that accept women equally with men."

"And you, Miss Felicia..."

"I graduated from Normal School last year. I was in my first year of teaching when news reached me of the Indian attack. Naturally, I was eager to return home as soon as possible. Aunt Winnifred insisted on making the journey with me, which I have appreciated over and over. She is very good company. Besides chaperoning me, she looks forward to supervising my father's recovery back to health."

Before Fletcher Crane could ask a more probing question, Felicia batted her long eyelashes and asked coyly, "And you, Captain, how did you come by those bars?"

"I . . . I ran away from home and a domineering father when I was sixteen. A friend and I joined the Army together. I admit that my driving force has been to prove that I'm more of a man than my father ever gave me credit for being—a common enlistment motive among the men circled around the campfire tonight."

Felicia followed his gaze to Carson.

"You haven't been home in . . ."

"Fifteen years."

Felicia shook her head. "It's hard for me to imagine such an angry separation within a family. I'd give anything to have my family united in one place again."

He continued as if he had not heard her comment. "I vowed that I would not go home until the scars forged on my back by my father's razor strap disappeared. I've come to realize that will never happen."

Felicia reached out and touched the Captain's arm. She wished it were his heart she could comfort.

"For my mother's sake, I have decided to return home for a visit after we complete this campaign. I no longer feel that I need to prove my worth to anyone, including my father."

They walked in silence, each trapped by his or her own thoughts.

Then, as the pair neared the place where they would part, Fletcher Crane stopped and gently turned Felicia toward him. She looked up into his face and winced as the moonlight beamed down upon the scar on his cheek. *Is his father responsible for that, too?*

"Felicia, we cannot dwell in the past. We have the future to look forward to. It is an act of God that brought us together in this unlikely place at this moment in time. Surely it was meant to be. It is up to us to make it count for something. Please, may I see you again?"

Felicia felt her knees weaken. Of course she wanted to see him again. But how or when?

"You seem troubled," he said quietly. "I should have guessed. A beautiful lady—you are promised?"

A blush washed over Felicia's cheeks. Hopefully the darkness hid her feelings from the tall officer pleading for her attention. "No, I am not spoken for..."

"Say no more. I am happier than I ever thought possible."

Later that cold autumn night, nestled under a layer of warm blankets, Felicia lay looking up at the dark storm clouds stealing silently across the rich orange face of the harvest moon.

Is the Lord warning us to be on the lookout for dark days ahead, or is He simply shutting off the bright light of heaven to better conceal us from our enemies?

It was a question too weighty for Felicia's bone-weary body to debate after the long, event-filled day and a surprisingly delicious and filling meal at the First Dragoons' campfire.

On this night, the last one of November, 1846, Felicia finally set aside her fear of night-stalkers. For the first time in weeks, after her evening prayers when her eyelids grew heavy, she allowed herself the luxury of drifting peacefully into dreamland. Felicia expected that the handsome Captain would be waiting for her there, just as she knew that he was waiting in the darkness beyond the glow of the campfire, his ice-green eyes watching over her as she slept.

The next sound Felicia remembered hearing was that of a bugle playing morning reveille. Her dawning thought was one of disappointment. Handsome Captain Crane had not come to her in her dreams. Perhaps their whole encounter was a fantasy and he was not real at all!

She closed her eyes again, retreating to that illusionary place somewhere between earth and heaven where young maidens build castles in the clouds. Felicia searched in vain for the officer who had slipped away from her last evening into the darkness, leaving behind the sweet memory of a whispered kiss against her ear.

It was then that she heard footsteps crushing her dream. They were striding purposefully toward her across the frost-tipped meadow.

"Good morning, Miss Felicia. It's 6 A.M. Time to rise and shine."

Felicia opened her eyes and sat up quickly. It hadn't been an illusion after all. Fletcher Crane was not only real, but he was standing above her and smiling down at her, his weariness having blown away with last evening's storm clouds.

Before she could utter more than her own "Good morning," the Captain interjected, "we haven't a moment to waste. Hurry and get ready. Even now your coach is waiting on the trail. A breakfast of freshly roasted quail and cold, wild melon is packed in your hamper and is already in the coach."

"Have we overslept?" she asked, looking around. Aunt Winnifred and Ophelia Jenkins were themselves just arising. Mr. Jenkins was nowhere in sight.

"No. We want to give you the longest head start possible on the Yumas. They cannot follow you through the pass as long as we block it. We hope the delay will fully discourage them from chasing after you later in the day."

"I don't understand. Aren't you going to San Diego also? Can't we travel together? I'm sure we wouldn't be any trouble..."

Crane smiled warmly at her. "It is everything to me that you want us to be together, even a day longer. But unfortunately, that is impossible."

"Why, Fletcher, why?"

"Our military equipment cannot make it through the narrow pass. That is why we stopped here so early in the day yesterday. Had we covered our usual distance, you and I would never have met.

"Within the hour we will begin our march to the north and around these mountain peaks to a place where, we are told, the springs run warm as bathwater."

While they talked, Crane helped Felicia fold her blankets and gather her things. Then while he and another officer carried the ladies' belongings to the waiting coach, the women disappeared behind the boulders for a last face-washing.

A few minutes later the ladies were hurrying up the path to the coach. The driver and Shotgun Sam were already seated high on their bench and the horses were prancing in place, eager to be on their way in the cool of the morning.

Fletcher Crane stepped to Felicia's side the moment she appeared at the trail's edge. He took her arm and hurriedly escorted her to the coach door.

"Don't forget me, my Felicia," he begged softly. "You will hear from me the moment we reach San Diego—victorious." Then soberly he inquired of her, "May I have something of yours to encourage me in battle? A scarf? A handkerchief...?"

Quickly Felicia pulled her mother's lace handkerchief from her pocket and laid it in the Captain's palm. He wrapped his fingers possessively around hers.

"Until we meet again, you are in my every thought."

"And you, in my every prayer," she replied in a quick breath.

Crane opened his mouth to say something, then paused and shook his head as if to cancel his thoughts.

Before Felicia could coax him, Crane encircled her tiny waist with his large hands and lifted her effortlessly into the coach.

Felicia ignored Mrs. Jenkins' disapproving look. She turned quickly to Fletcher Crane as the door shut between them.

"How will you know where to find me?" she asked through the open window.

"In a pueblo of only 350 people, there can reside only one beautiful Felicia Maria Worthington," he called back, his face beaming.

Felicia's head spun. Suddenly the coach bolted forward. It was too late to reply.

What have I done? Felicia's heart ached with her own deception. *I'll not deny my heritage ever again—whatever the cost!* she vowed.

Felicia waved back at the officer with the ice-green eyes—a man she was certain she would never see again.

3

*F*elicia lost track of time as the coach made its way over the serpentine mountain trail bordered by fields of wild oats and mustard weed, watched over by ageless sycamores and spreading oaks.

The sky grew grayer as the day wore on. It was no longer easy for Felicia to doze off, freeing her mind to wander among the clouds hand-in-hand with a handsome officer of the First Dragoons. It was getting too cold for that. Keeping warm in the drafty coach took Felicia's full concentration.

"From the parched desert to the threat of snow in almost a day's time. It escapes me why anyone wants to fight over this unpredictable land," scoffed Ophelia Jenkins. She pulled out another lap robe and spread it over her knees.

It was then that Felicia noticed that Mrs. Jenkins had returned her wedding ring to her left hand. *Evidently she believes we've outrun the Indians for good. I pray that she's right.*

It was not much longer before they heard the tap-tap of raindrops hitting the roof. Immediately the driver pulled under a limb of an old oak tree at the side of the trail.

"Are we stopping for the night?" Jenkins called up to the driver.

"No, Sir. We're just putting on our raingear. We've got a lot of ground to cover before this muddy trail becomes impassable."

A moment later they were on their way again. By now the rain was pouring down, blinding their vision of even the near horizon.

Was it on that afternoon, or during the next afternoon's rain, that the driver drove along a narrow ridgetop, then slowed to a stop at a naturally formed overlook? Felicia could not remember. Days were beginning to blur together. Her journal read Thursday, December 2, 1846.

Felicia gazed out of the window. The sheer drop below them made it seem as if they were hanging from a basket in the sky, so tiny was the world below. Even the date seemed suspended in time.

The rain let up at that moment, and all four passengers quickly stepped out of the coach on its far side.

"Caution now," the driver warned. "Don't come

around from behind the protection of the carriage and get too near the edge. The wind will blow you over and down into San Pascual Valley below."

The group huddled together well back from the precipice.

"It's beautiful!" exclaimed Felicia. "Look at that river snaking through the middle of the lush green vegetation. You can see where it's overflowing its banks in a couple of places. What a geography lesson!"

"That overflow's caused by rain runoff from the mountains," offered Shotgun Sam. "Give it another month and the river could yawn wide enough to cover most of the valley floor. It's happened before."

Felicia's voice held a trace of awe. "The beauty of God's handiwork—the mountain walls jutting almost straight up appear to be held together by millions of white marbles!"

"Those marbles, Miss Worthington," continued Sam, "are huge granite boulders. After a heavy rain, some have been known to pull loose and roll free. As we get closer to them, you'll see that they are many times the size of our stagecoach."

"Closer?" inquired Aunt Winnifred. "We're going down there?"

The driver grinned. "We sure are, Ma'am." Then he untied the dirty red bandana from around his neck and spread it open. He placed it on top of a trailside boulder and weighted its corners with smaller rocks.

He stepped back from the edge, seeming rather pleased with himself. "It's an old Indian trick. When we get down in the middle of that valley, you can look back up here and see where we started our descent."

"The valley floor must not be too difficult a place to get to," commented Aunt Winnifred. "See that ribbon of smoke rising below? It looks to be coming from a settlement partially hidden by that large cluster of trees."

They all looked in the direction she pointed.

"Civilization at last!" Mrs. Jenkins was overjoyed.

"You're right about that, Ma'am," agreed Sam. "It's an Indian village. The smoke is coming from wigwams."

Mrs. Jenkins was about to faint on the spot until Sam added with a twinkle in his watery-gray eyes, "They're a peaceful tribe—resettled here when the mission closed."

How does he know whether they're peaceful or not when under the cover of darkness? Maybe they are the savages who raided Rancho El Camino.

"Everyone back into the coach," called the driver. "We've got to make it through San Pascual Valley and up the far hill to Rancho Rincon del Diablo before nightfall."

"Finally a true, civilized respite on this endless journey," sighed Ophelia Jenkins. Then, almost as an afterthought, she asked, "What does Rincon del Diablo mean?"

The old codger spat his chewing tobacco out on the ground, then replied evenly, "The Devil's Corner."

Their journey through the picturesque valley was uneventful. Thankfully so, thought Felicia as she enjoyed the strong, rich colors of the fertile landscape and boulder-cropped, purple mountains that towered above them.

Once they wound up out of the lowland it was not long before the driver called back, "Ahead on that wooded hillside is the *hacienda* of Don Juan Bautista Alvarado, where we will be welcomed for the night.''

As promised, a few moments later they came into view of a large, whitewashed adobe hacienda with a hand-hewn shake roof. Even as they approached the main drive, it was evident to them that Rancho Rincon del Diablo was abandoned. Weeds overran the yard and paint had chipped away from the exposed face of the mud-block home.

The ladies walked along the front veranda while the men looked around back for some sign of life. Felicia ran her finger across a windowpane. ''Real glass,'' she commented.

''I count six rooms,'' Aunt Winnifred said, stepping to her side.

''Oh, Aunt Winn, I feel as if I'm finally home. I didn't realize how much I missed the texture of adobe, the beauty of the arched arcades, and the smell of the 'cup of gold' flowering at the eaves.''

''If you give your hand to a certain captain in the U.S. Army, you'll not be sweeping clay floors in the West or wearing hibiscus blossoms in your hair. It will be wood floors and straw bonnets in a cottage along the Eastern seaboard—which is an idyllic combination for those of us who cotton to a civilized lifestyle.''

''You know how I love Boston, the smell of the ocean spray crashing against the rocks and the caw of the gulls floating on the air current overhead.''

''I know, Dear. You're the best clam-digger in the family.''

''It's just that I feel in my heart of hearts that California is where I belong. My roots are here.

Do you understand, Aunt Winn?''

"Of course I understand. . ." Her voice trailed off.

"What is it you're not saying?" Felicia pried softly but insistently.

Aunt Winnifred smiled and said, "You read me well, my sweet." She slipped her arm through Felicia's and they began to stroll away from the main house.

"Captain Crane is the first of many suitors you will have while visiting your father. Here we do not have the resources to examine their backgrounds as we would Boston-bred gentlemen. And," she added tactfully, "your father may be too ill to advise us."

"But, Aunt Winn, I'm not looking for a husband, here or in Boston."

"How well I know. You've discouraged the most eligible bachelors in the city, if not in the whole state." She patted her niece's hand affectionately and added, "It's time to soften your heart, Felicia dear, as you are far beyond the average age of today's brides."

"That doesn't concern me," Felicia replied with an independent air. "I'll never marry for convenience—you know that. I intend to do as my father did and marry only for love."

Aunt Winnifred was quiet for a moment, then confided, "I was as strong-willed as you at your age. I never found love, but what I did do was pass up several respectable, Christian suitors. Any one of them would have provided well and given me my own children and grandchildren to love. Now, in my middle years, I would have had a welcome source of companionship."

Felicia stopped and faced her beloved aunt. She saw herself reflected in the tears filling Aunt

Winnifred's hazel eyes.

"What I'm saying, my darling Felicia, is that the most important quality in a husband is his love for Jesus Christ and his eagerness to honor Christ by living according to His Word. In the scheme of life it really doesn't matter whether he is a Bostonian or a Californio, whether he has a commission in the U.S. Army or captains a sailing vessel, whether his hair is the color of sun-drenched cornsilk or even if he is bald."

Her aunt's words struck a nerve of truth. "Aunt Winn, your point is well-taken," she uttered. "I know the color of Captain Crane's eyes but not the spiritual tone of his heart. I should not have encouraged his suit until I questioned . . ."

Suddenly her mind was back at the moment of their parting. "The coach was pulling away. There was no time to stand on propriety . . ." she reflected aloud.

Felicia remembered, too, that Fletcher Crane started, then decided to withhold comment on her pledge to keep him "in every prayer."

The two women retraced their steps back to the hacienda.

Had they been blessed with more time together, she wondered, would she have queried Captain Crane about his relationship with God? Probably not. Aunt Winnifred was right: Her priorities were not in order.

Felicia's musings were cut short by the return of the men. Shotgun Sam headed straight for the horses while their driver approached the ladies, now gathering on the veranda.

"We found an old Indian living back among the trees. He seems to be the unofficial caretaker of the place."

"What happened to the Don and his family?" Felicia asked.

"According to what I could make out from the old Indian, who was half-afraid of us and doesn't speak much English, the Don died several months ago. He had six children, all of whom have scattered. I couldn't make out what happened to the Dona. Our communication broke down at that point."

"Do you think it's safe for us to stay the night here?" inquired Ophelia Jenkins.

"Yes," her husband answered. "Even I understood that we are welcome to make ourselves at home. The hacienda is unlocked. The old fella took us through it by way of the kitchen. Neat as a pin. He must sweep the floors every day. There are dishes in the cupboards, and pots and pans..."

"What about food?" Ophelia interrupted her husband in her hurry to get to the meat of the matter.

"He's wringing a couple of chickens' necks for us right now," grinned the driver. "And if you ladies know how to fix winter squash, I'd say we'll be having a right-fine meal tonight."

"Chicken for dinner tonight means eggs for breakfast in the morning—if your man didn't kill the only two laying hens," teased Felicia.

"I promise you a California-sized meal in the morning before we hit the trail and aim straight toward the Pacific Ocean. Another couple of days and this journey will be history." With that said, the driver led the group into the hacienda.

The front door had no more than closed behind them when a flash of lightning creased the sky and the rumble of thunder filled the room. By the time the six of them sat down to dinner, rain was pummeling the rooftop.

They looked at one another. Felicia extended her arms. Without a word the others did the same. They joined hands and bowed their heads. It was the first time in all their weeks cramped together that the group prayed as one.

"Thank You, Lord, for this blessed house to protect us from the rain. Thank You, Lord, for this food now set before us according to Your goodness. Thank You, Lord, for watching over us during this long journey. And finally, Lord, we thank You especially for . . . each other."

Mrs. Jenkins sniffled. The driver cleared his throat. Sam snorted. Jenkins wiped his eyes with the back of his hand and Aunt Winnifred smiled.

We all hunger for the same thing, don't we, Lord? How sad that each of us has kept his candle under a bushel until now—when the trip is nearly over. All along we've been "family" and didn't know it. What joy, what unity we've missed! I'm actually sorry that we have so little time left to get to "know" one another. Aunt Winn is right—I must let my light shine!

By noon the next day Felicia could smell the ocean salt in the breeze coming off the Pacific, still twenty miles west. Not until they had passed south across San Bernardo Rancho to Los Penasquitos Creek and headed for Soledad Valley did she truly realize that she was almost home. By this time tomorrow she would be in her father's arms!

The words of the *majordomo's* letter flashed in front of her one more time. ". . . I report the Don's declining health . . . please come with haste before it is too late."

So much had happened on each day of the journey that Felicia had not had the time to brood over the awful possibility of arriving "too late."

Panic washed over her.

Dear Lord, please...

Then, as quick as last evening's bolt of lightning, a new concern struck. *What if Father has died of his wounds? Will his staff, his rancheros, still be there? Or will they have abandoned the beautiful hacienda and allowed the rancho to fall to ruin like Rancho Rincon del Diablo?*

Her mind sped on, creating its own strangling web of "what ifs." *What if the property has slipped into the hands of the enemy? How would I, a single woman, go about reclaiming my rightful inheritance?*

Then another shocking revelation hit Felicia. *Enemy? Who is the enemy? On which side does, or did, my father stand on the U.S.-Mexican War?*

Felicia scolded herself. *I should have come home the minute I graduated from college. I should not have taken a position in the East. Surely teachers are needed on the Frontier. There is so much my father needed to teach me before...*

"Make room! Make room!" The shouted order cut the air with the coldness of steel.

Suddenly the carriage jumped the trail and plowed to a bouncing halt in the middle of a rocky field.

"What the...?" exclaimed Jenkins.

All four peered wide-eyed out the window. There, passing only a few feet from them, was the dreaded army of Californios!

General Pico marched near the front, among the

men with gay pennants fluttering from medieval lances. The soldiers wore the traditional rich and ornamented costumes of the Dons, with leather cuirasses to protect their bodies, and *serapes* draped over one shoulder. A few carried the old leather shields displaying their Castilian heraldry. Their mounts stepped smartly. Both men and beasts looked fresh and well-fed.

The entire army paraded by without one of the men looking aside. It was as if the dust-covered carriage was of absolutely no consequence.

It was Aunt Winnifred who kept her wits and counted the number of men. "Seventy-five in all," she announced as the last man passed.

Felicia's heart sank. General Kearny's bedraggled forces were no match for this proud band of men.

The main body of the army was fifty yards down the trail before the stagecoach driver picked up the reins. Felicia sensed that he too was caught off-guard by the snub given them by the hot-tempered corps of fighters.

As they eased out onto the trail once again, Felicia began to talk in an effort to take her mind off the knot in the pit of her stomach.

"Julius, you asked me earlier about the Californios."

Obviously pleased that Felicia called him by his given name, the man responded in an eager tone. "Yes, I am confused as to whom the United States is actually fighting. I'm not even sure General Kearny knows."

Felicia raised her eyebrows, surprised by Jenkins' bold remark. "Let me give you the same overview I gave my students before I set out on this trip, flavored with additional insight supplied by Captain Crane, following his discussions with Kit Carson."

Jenkins nodded and Felicia began.

"Even under Spanish rule, California was a remote territory subject to little direct influence of the King or the Church. Mexico's revolution against Spain further lessened the fragile ties of domination from Mexico City. In 1832, Mexico cut itself loose from a costly burden by secularizing the missions of California and releasing thousands of Indians to become homeless wanderers.

"Many of the missionaries remained at their posts doing what they could to help the few Christian Indians who elected to remain at the missions, where many of them had been born and had lived all their lives. Besides, they were sorely needed to maintain the fields, gardens, and stock.

"By 1836, the situation with the majority of Indians—Dieguenos, Luisenos, Cahuillas, and Yumas—had become explosive. Imagine the tiny adobe settlement of 350 people backed against the sea by 10,000 angry Indians!

"During this same time, fanned by the upheaval of their own revolution, several successive Mexican governors awarded vast tracts of mission land to relatives and friends, as well as to American traders and settlers who would first file for Mexican citizenship."

"Traitors—selling their birthright for a plot of land!" scoffed Jenkins. "Shoot them with the rest of the enemy!"

Felicia held up her hand to silence Jenkins. "Wait until I finish before judging."

The man closed his mouth, but his eyes still seethed with rage. Felicia continued, controlling her tone to sound as neutral as possible.

"It is a common belief that Mexico's tenuous hold over California ended with the decline of the missions. The land was up for grabs, so to speak.

"For the relatives of the governors, the land gift was a reward for service and an effort to stave off a land war in the future. As for the Americans, they realized that Mexican citizenship was a temporary passport to owning land in an independent state. Frankly, many thought England would get into the fight over California."

"What you're saying, Felicia, is that not all Californios are fighting for Mexico." Jenkins' voice was calmer now.

"Right. Some dons are United States supporters. Some are in favor of an independent state. It's the same with the Indians. Some tribes are angry with Mexico's treatment of them. Others are frightened over the United States' intervention. Some, like the Yumas, just want to make bad medicine for everyone."

Jenkins sighed, "You cannot tell the enemy by his uniform. You cannot even tell by his skin color!"

Felicia smiled and nodded. She was exhausted. She leaned back in her corner and rested her head against a pillow. The salt air was growing heavier as they neared the sea, the lulling salt air, the beautiful sea...

Felicia slipped into dreamland as easily as a wave slides across a sandy shoreline. She floated to that place where, by the light of the moon, she and Fletcher Crane had said their goodnight two evenings ago.

She stood breathlessly close to him. Shyly, she reached up and gently touched the scar on his cheek. He did not wince. Instead, he took her hand in his and kissed each delicate fingertip in turn, all the while loving her with his intense, green eyes.

Then the handsome officer picked her up in his arms and swung her around and around and . . .

"Felicia! Wake up!" Aunt Winnifred's voice rippled through the clouds, causing her dream man to fade before her eyes. She reached for him but it was too late. He was gone!

"Felicia! Felicia!" Her aunt's voice sounded desperate.

Felicia opened her eyes and looked into her aunt's frightened face.

"Felicia, we've stopped again. This time we do have something to fear. We've been ambushed!" Aunt Winnifred pointed out the window.

Felicia leaned across her aunt and gazed out the window. Was she still dreaming?

From where she sat she could see six Indians, dressed much like the Californios, holding rifles on their driver and Shotgun Sam.

"We've got nothing of value," she heard Sam snarl. "We don't even have a strongbox aboard. You've got the wrong stagecoach, boys."

"We have the right stagecoach."

Felicia turned quickly to see where the deep voice was coming from.

It came from a man riding out from the stand of pines bordering the trail. Felicia could not take her eyes off the dark-skinned man. He was dressed like a . . . Don!

He had on short breeches extending to the knee, ornamented with silver lace at the bottom. The leggings below were made of the softest deerskin. They were tied at the knee by a silk cord with tassels.

He wore a bolero-type jacket, with filigree buttons of silver. His suit was brown. The silk cummerbund around his waist was red and his silk shirt was white. His hat—exactly like the one her father wore—had to have been imported from Peru. It was stiff, with a flat, wide brim, under which his long black sideburns showed.

But it was the trappings on his white stallion that took her breath away. The saddle was silver-mounted and embroidered with silver, as was the bridle. The reins, made with the finest hair from a horse's mane, were connected every few inches with a link of pure silver.

Under the saddle was the *anqueta*, of leather, in a half-moon shape covering the horse's hind-quarter. It was heavily decorated. The under-side was of sheepskin. The stirrups were large and inlaid with silver also. In addition, the spur straps were woven throughout with silver thread.

"Glory be!" exclaimed Ophelia. "He looks like a king!"

The mysterious rider rode closer. His silver trap-pings commanded their own respect, as they glistened in the afternoon sun, ricocheting off the deep blue ocean now at the backs of Felicia and the others.

"Put down your rifles, men. I trust we'll not have to use them."

"You're right about that, Sir. We've got nothing of value aboard," snapped Sam. "If it's precious jewels you're looking for..."

"That I am," the stranger interrupted in a loud, firm voice. "I have come to claim the most precious jewel in the land. I am here to collect my bride—the beautiful Senorita Las Flores!''

4

*F*elicia gasped. Sheer black fright enveloped her.

"Oh, no!" Shotgun Sam exclaimed with relish. "Look at your reflection in that silver you're sporting and you'll see a fool! We've no Senorita Las Flores aboard."

Immediately the Indians raised their rifles.

"He's serious!" Jenkins whispered in astonishment. "He really thinks we'd travel with a Mexican woman!"

"Let's get out so he can see that we're not hiding

anyone." Ophelia Jenkins reached for the door handle.

Aunt Winnifred instantly put her hand over the other woman's. "We'd better wait. Sam is in charge. He'll tell us when or if . . ."

"This probably isn't their first ambush," Felicia sighed, trying to sound nonchalant.

The subject was not debatable, for the next words they heard were in the form of a stern order.

"Open the carriage door. I demand to see my bride."

"Wait!" Sam admonished. "By whose command is the order given?"

The Don took off his hat and swept it low. "By me, Sir." He spoke with cool authority. "It is the command of Don Andres Santiago."

Felicia heard Shotgun Sam shifting on the bench seat above them. Was he reaching for a gun or biding for time?

"Here is our manifest." Sam handed down a leather folder to one of the Don's men. Before the Indian took two steps toward his master, the Don stopped him with a cold glare.

"Look at it," Sam encourged. "You'll see that we have four passengers—three Yankee ladies and one Yankee gentleman."

The arrogant stranger made no move to receive the manifest. A twitch at his jawline warned Felicia of his building impatience.

"Suit yourself," Sam shrugged. "Either way, we have a schedule to keep. It's time for us to move on." He motioned to the driver to pick up the reins.

"*Caballeros!* Open the carriage door and assist my bride." The Don's command could be postponed no longer.

Felicia's body trembled. "Who is he? How does he know me?" she mouthed to Aunt Winn as the Jenkinses climbed out first.

"I have no idea, Dear. God go with you. Your father's men will be on your trail the moment we arrive. As a Worthington, I promise you that!"

Aunt Winn followed the Jenkinses from the carriage.

Felicia bowed her head and prayed silently, *Guard and protect me from this devil, Lord. Please do not allow harm to come to the others because of me. And please, Lord, watch over my father...*

Aunt Winn stuck her head through the carriage door. "Felicia, come! The Don grows more impatient."

Felicia stepped to the door of the coach. She paused, and with her chin held high she looked directly into the dark, insolent eyes of the stranger commanding her obedience.

Everyone was silent.

"As you see, Don Santiago, we do not have the lady you seek. Your apology, *Senor,* and we will forgive the entire inconvenience."

Sam's remark made no impression on the Don. His attention was riveted on Felicia.

Felicia stepped to the ground. Then all eyes shifted from her to the Don.

"Good afternoon, Senorita Las Flores," the Don said, tipping his hat. "You are more beautiful than I expected."

"You...you are the woman he is looking for?" Julius Jenkins asked incredulously.

"I am Felicia Maria Worthington Las Flores," Felicia responded proudly, her eyes still on the Don's. "How this man came by that information

I do not know. I have neither seen nor heard of this Don 'imposter' before.'' Felicia's dark eyes snapped with the sharpness of her words.

"A woman with fire! I like that." Don Andres smiled easily, his teeth strikingly white against his olive-skinned face. "I am well-pleased with my purchase," he said, clipping the stallion with his silver spurs.

"Purchase!" Felicia gasped.

Her head started to spin. She closed her eyes and reached out toward Aunt Winn as the earth began to slip away beneath her feet.

Suddenly Felicia's feet were no longer touching the ground! She half-opened her eyes to see the Don's sharply chiseled face close to hers as he scooped her up onto the silver-ladened saddle and set her down in front of him. He cradled her with a strong arm, her limp body molding easily against his broad chest.

Before half-conscious Felicia could utter a word of protest, the Don shot a command to his men in Spanish, then spurred his horse forward. Moments later Felicia and her abductor were riding like the wind cross-country on the Don's galloping steed.

"Put me down! Put me down this instant!" Felicia ordered the moment her head stopped reeling.

Her demand only served to spur the stallion on faster, forcing Felicia to cling more tightly to her captor for fear of being thrown to the ground.

Finally the Don slowed the huge animal to a trot, then to a walk. Only then did Felicia try to wiggle loose and drop free.

"You are harder to break than Sky Cloud." Don Andres touched a spur to the horse's flank once again. Sky Cloud charged ahead.

This time the Don did not hold her closely, and Felicia felt herself slip a little with each length the horse galloped. Edging toward panic, she threw her arms around the Don's chest. Her hands did not meet across his muscular back!

"I'm falling!" Felicia screamed at him in terror.

Instantly the Don's arm tightened around her protectively—pulling her so close that she was forced to breath in rhythm with her handsome, dark-skinned abductor.

She stole a glance at her "devil in Don's clothing" in time to see his lips curve into a roguish smile.

"It is up to you, Felicia, whether we continue at this breakneck speed or slow to a more comfortable pace. Our destination remains the same."

So close was his mouth to hers that his breath brushed her face, tickling her long lashes. A rush of excitement shot through her body.

Felicia looked up again—this time long enough to study the clear-cut lines of the Don's profile.

Don Andres' thick black sideburns were flecked at the lowest edge with white. He wore a thin moustache, like a "real" Don would wear.

"Who are you, really? What do you want of me?"

He did not answer. Felicia resigned herself to silence.

Before long the Don veered Sky Cloud toward a grove of oaks. Once under its shelter, Don Santiago reined in his stallion. In the unexpected silence Felicia heard the sound of rushing water nearby.

The Don dismounted near the edge of a heavily cobblestoned creek, then reached up for Felicia. She slipped her arms around his neck and a moment later she was floating in his arms.

The Don set her down carefully, keeping his arms encircled around her a moment longer than necessary. His brows furrowed as his eyes searched hers intently.

Felicia was determined that her eyes would tell him the same as he had told her—nothing! Still, she could not control the sudden quickening of her heart. She took a deep, unsteady breath and stepped back.

Don Andres took her by the hand and smiled. "You'll not escape me, my Felicia." He led her to a fallen log along the river's edge and motioned for her to sit down.

"You won't get away with this, you know," she said. "My father's *vaqueros* will be hot on our trail before nightfall."

"Wrong on two counts."

"How dare you..."

"First of all, the stagecoach will not reach San Diego until late tomorrow, allowing that it passes through enemy lines without delay. Then, someone would have to meet the stage and then backtrack almost twenty miles, crossing enemy lines again to Rancho El Camino with the news of the ambush.

"Today is Friday, December third. It would be late Saturday night, at the very earliest, before word could reach the rancho. War or no war, weekends are *fiesta* days. A tracking party of caballeros could not be gathered before dawn Monday, December sixth."

Felicia's heart sank. He was right and she knew

it. "What's the other count?" she asked deject-
edly, her eyes beginning to mist.

"Your aunt is not on that stage. She's close
behind us with my men and a horse-drawn
carreta containing your trunks and handcases. You two will be reunited by nightfall."

Felicia's mouth opened in surprise. The mist
became tears that rolled unchecked down
her cheeks. "How can I believe you?" she
asked.

"What choice do you have? Besides, I am not
the ogre I appear to be. Come, it's time to ride on.
It is a short distance to my hacienda at Rancho del
Dios, where a delicious dinner awaits us. Tonight
you will dine on more than roast chicken and
winter squash."

"How did you know...?" But it was too late.
The masquerading Don, who was becoming more
of an enigma every moment, was heading toward
the creek to reclaim his horse.

*Psychic powers are the work of Satan. I will
not marry a man possessed of the devil. Purchased
me, indeed! I am not a commodity. I am my father's
daughter. My father—what about my father? Is
he alive... or dead? If dead, by whose hand?*

Felicia stared at the mystery man coming toward
her now, leading his white stallion. Was he a
murderer, too?

A cold chill ran up her spine and collided with
the strange warmth of excitement racing through
her body.

Felicia was hopelessly confused.

5

*F*elicia awakened to the gentle sound of raindrops splattering against the windowpanes. She refused to open her eyes for fear that the down-softness surrounding her would disappear with the dream that she and Aunt Winnifred were nestled in a giant, hand-carved bed in a tapestry-draped bedroom of a spacious adobe hacienda.

The splattering soon became pounding, and Felicia's troubled curiosity increased with the intensity of the rain.

Slowly she opened her eyes and looked around. The tapestries still hung from ceiling to floor at the three windows in the room. The lace canopy overhead was held in place by hand-carved mahogany posts. Felicia rubbed her fingertips over the comforter under which she lay. It was not a dream cloud; it was real.

Fully awake now, she sat up and saw that Aunt Winnifred was indeed sleeping peacefully beside her.

There was a light knock on the door. Even so, it awakened her aunt.

"Who do you think it is?" Felicia whispered haltingly.

"I don't know, Dear," her aunt replied sleepily. "I suggest you ask."

"Aunt Winn, you're not afraid of anything. I wish I were more like you."

"Fear gives glory to Satan," Aunt Winn replied, taking off her flannel nightcap and setting her carrot-colored curls free.

Hearing a noise outside the door, Felicia called out cautiously, "Who is it?"

Felicia watched the doorknob turn. The door pushed slightly open. She held her breath and waited.

Suddenly the small face of an Indian maiden peeked around the door. "May I come in, Senorita?"

"Of course," smiled Felicia, throwing back the comforter and stepping gingerly onto a hand-woven Mexican rug.

The girl entered the room and curtsied. She had black, stringy hair the color of coal and dark eyes the size of tea saucers. Felicia guessed the young girl to be no more than eleven years of age.

"Your breakfast is ready, Senorita, whenever it pleases you."

"Thank you," Felicia smiled. "What is your name?"

"Fawn Eyes," she replied meekly, "is what my Indian name means in English."

"You speak English very well."

Felicia picked up her hairbrush and began running the stiff bristles through her silky long tresses.

"Please, sit down, Senorita, and I will brush your hair for you. I am to be your personal maid."

Felicia's eyes brightened. "Thank you, Fawn Eyes. I appreciate the majordomo's thoughtfulness, although I will not be here at Rancho del Dios long enough for you to do much."

Felicia settled herself on a velvet-cushioned stool and handed the Indian girl the delicately inlaid brush, a treasured heirloom of her own mother's.

"It was Don Santiago himself who chose me," Fawn Eyes said proudly. "He instructed me not to let you out of my sight until your wedding."

Felicia felt the color drain from her face. She opened her mouth, but before she could speak, Aunt Winn's eyes cautioned her to keep still. Then her aunt walked briskly to Felicia's trunk and pulled out the first dress she saw.

"Here, child," Aunt Winn ordered sweetly, "run and press this immediately so that the Senorita will have something appropriate to wear to breakfast."

As soon as Fawn Eyes left the room Aunt Winn warned, "Remember that walls have ears and everyone here on the rancho is loyal to the man who has kidnapped Don Las Flores' daughter and sister."

"A real Don—a kidnapper! Who would believe it? We must find a way to escape. We cannot stay here another night, let alone until a mythological wedding. The Don may be the law on the rancho, but not even Don Andres Santiago can force me into an unwanted marriage!"

"I agree! And I didn't believe for a minute the Don's promise last night at dinner that he intends to return us to Rancho El Camino today."

Felicia put her hand on her aunt's shoulder. "Do you believe he told us the truth when he said that Father is alive and knows of our pending arrival?"

"No, I don't," Aunt Winn sighed hopelessly. "If Don Juan Las Flores were alive, he would have sent his own men to intercept the stage or to meet us in San Diego." She patted her niece's hand. "I'm sorry, Felicia," she continued. "I don't see how it could be otherwise."

Felicia replied in a weak defense, "It's turned out that he is who he claimed to be—Don Andres Santiago. Also, he reunited us, as he promised, and has treated us like royal houseguests. I want so much to believe him when he says Father is alive."

"Felicia!" her aunt's eyes sparked. "That man ambushed our stagecoach, abducted us, and is now holding us prisoners. A comfortable bed is not freedom! You are too trusting, my dear niece."

Fawn Eyes returned with Felicia's freshly pressed dress. She placed it on the bed while she helped Felicia into her taffeta petticoat with the velvet trim. The dress itself was a red-and-green plaid muslin. The neckline was wide and low. The short sleeves were made of two scalloped ruffles, with the same ruffle repeated as a flounce all around the hem of the full skirt.

By the time Fawn Eyes had tied the sash at the back of Felicia's small waist and buttoned Aunt Winn's last button, the two were more than a little hungry for breakfast.

Fawn Eyes directed the ladies to the dining room, where a beautifully prepared buffet of fruit, eggs, meat, and hot muffins awaited them on the sideboard. Fawn Eyes disappeared at the nod of the housekeeper's head.

Felicia picked up a ripe orange, absentmindedly testing the skin with one of her thumbnails.

"There's enough fresh fruit here to keep a whole army free of scurvy," whispered Aunt Winn.

A twinge of guilt surged through Felicia as Captain Crane's hunger-drawn face appeared before her mind's eye. "I wish General Kearny's forces would charge through the door about now. We'd be rescued and they would get a hearty breakfast."

"The First Dragoons are proud patriots. I believe they would prefer hunting the Mexican Army and choking down hardtack to barging in on the Don's Old World hospitality."

Aunt Winn's attempt at levity did nothing to extinguish the rekindled longing within Felicia's breast.

Only when they were seated at the formal dining table did Felicia have nerve to ask of the serving maid, "Is the Don joining us for breakfast?"

"No, Senorita, he left the rancho early this morning. We don't know when he will return."

Felicia and her aunt exchanged quick glances. Perhaps they did have time to plot an escape. They ate hurriedly, then excused themselves, saying that since the rain had stopped they wished to get out for some fresh air.

The two waited in the front hall while Fawn Eyes fetched their capes and bonnets from their room.

Once dressed for the weather, Felicia met the questioning eyes of the majordomo with her own query: "In which direction is the chapel?"

He smiled and pointed to the path leading through the oaks off the north end of the long, tiled arcade.

As soon as the two were out of sight of their adobe prison, Felicia suggested, "Let's find the stable first. We need to discover what might be available here for getaway transportation."

Aunt Winn nodded in agreement and the two took the first fork they found in the path.

However, the structure at the path's end was not a stable. Felicia and Aunt Winn approached the deserted building and peered through a dirty glass window along the east side.

"It looks like one big room," said Felicia, standing on her tiptoes. "Let's see if the door is locked."

The two managed to push the weather-warped door open enough to slip through. "It's a schoolhouse!" Felicia exclaimed. "Look, there are the benches pushed into the corner. Over there is the teacher's desk and a stack of slates."

Felicia walked over to a cupboard in the farthest corner. Its shelves were lined with books. "Look, Aunt Winn, a copy of *McGuffey's Reader*. And here's a copy of Noah Webster's 'blue-backed' *Speller*. What a treasure store!"

"Another mystery—a well-stocked schoolroom falling into disrepair. Another crime against the Don!"

"We won't be able to tell anyone about it or our abduction if we don't get away from here soon. Let's find that stable," Felicia suggested anxiously. She quickly led the way out of the schoolhouse and back up the path to the fork.

The second fork did lead eventually to the stable, although they both realized they had come by a circuitous route. A more direct path from the hacienda would have to be discovered before their escape attempt.

They approached the stable, pretending as little interest in their surroundings as possible, in case they were being watched. They strolled quietly past a row of stalls. Felicia counted several well-marked mares, geldings, and stallions.

The two rounded a corner of the building and stopped. Felicia pondered their predicament, tapping a beautifully manicured finger against her cheek.

"Plenty of magnificent horseflesh. All of it too fine for rancho work. These must be the Don's personal mounts. The caballeros undoubtedly stable their horses at another location closer to their bunkhouses."

"So? As horse thieves, we might as well steal the best."

"There's only one problem..."

"May I help you, Senorita?"

The two women whipped around. A weathered old Indian, clutching a finely honed hatchet, stood not five feet from them.

His face remained expressionless as he asked, "Are you looking for something?"

"Yes...yes we are. We admired the Don's spectacular silver trappings. We were hoping to get a closer look at them. Is that possible?"

The old Indian nodded. Then with one flick of his arm he sent the weapon sailing toward the nearest tree trunk. A hard thud and it held fast.

The women sighed in relief.

The old man led them to a locked tackroom within the feed barn. They watched as he reached underneath a nail keg to retrieve the key that fitted the heavy lock. Felicia smiled at their good fortune.

The two spent several uncomfortable minutes admiring the gold and silver bridles, saddles, spurs, and other frightfully expensive trappings that required hours of weekly hand-polishing.

Finally, after admiring the last saddle in the tack-room, Felicia and her aunt hurried from the stable grounds.

"That was not a place to have the Don ride in and find us," said Felicia.

Aunt Winn scowled worriedly. "He's bound to come home soon. We'd better get back to the main house."

"You're right. However, you go ahead. I think I should take an extra minute and find the chapel. Since that's where we're supposed to be, we'd better know what it looks like."

During the next few minutes Felicia found the summer kitchen, the tile bathhouse, the smokehouse, and several other outbuildings that she could not immediately identify.

There was something else that she could not reconcile—a feeling about the Indians on the place. First, there weren't any around to do all the things that needed to be done on a working rancho. Then there was the one Indian who seemed to always be around—five feet behind them when they least expected him. There was something familiar about that particular old Indian...

Suddenly, there it was, directly in front of her—the chapel. Painted stones edged the final fifty feet of the path to the entrance. Resplendent in freshly whitewashed adobe, the chapel looked much like the San Diego Mission the way she remembered it as a child: the cast-iron bell hanging above the arched doorway, the red tile roof, the deep-set windows, even the vines entwined in the bell tower—architecture reminiscent of her Spanish heritage. It beckoned "Come unto me..."

And she did.

One step over the threshhold and Felicia knew she was in the temple of the Lord. A row of wall brackets held tall, lighted candles that cast a warmth the length of the chancel. The gold-leaf-encrusted altar glittered—caught in the light streaming down from the stained-glass window crowned above it. A dozen rows of hand-carved wooden pews sat on a mirror-polished Mexican floor tile. A handcrafted Mexican carpet ran down the narrow center aisle. Freshly picked red roses in brass vases filled the niches on each side of the entry where she stood.

Felicia slowly and reverently walked down the center aisle to the front of the chapel. Only then did she notice an oversized open Bible resting on a raised wrought-iron stand to her left.

She walked over to it and gazed down at the elaborate scrolling and hand-lettering of an anonymous Franciscan monk.

Her eyes scanned the page, coming to rest on the words of Psalm 140:

> Deliver me, O Lord, from the evil man;
> preserve me from the violent man,
> which imagine mischiefs in their heart;
> continually are they gathered together
> for war.

Felicia felt her spine tingle as she claimed David's prayer for her own.

She stepped back and entered the front pew. With sincere humbleness she lowered herself to her knees, bowed her head, and closed her eyes.

Father in heaven, deliver us from this evil man. Please aid our escape. Lead us safely to my father. . . .

Then suddenly—a familiar voice melded with her sacred meditation.

"What is the prayer of your desire, dear Felicia? Your petition is my command." Don Santiago's whispered words collided with those in her heart.

Felicia turned her head slowly to face the man she so wanted to believe.

Startled, she drew back. Only the dark, liquid eyes of the figure next to her were those of the Don's. The true identity of the man beside her was hidden by a shroudlike serape and the black mask of a Mexican *bandito!*

Felicia jumped to her feet and fled toward the side aisle.

The masked man grabbed her by the wrist and twisted her toward him. Then he pulled Felicia roughly to him and met her protesting mouth with his own in a long, hard kiss.

6

Wherever the Don went that morning, he had used a buckboard. Felicia saw it out of the corner of her eye from her place at the dining table during their late luncheon. It was standing under an old oak tree behind the hacienda with the horse still hitched to it.

Felicia ate her hot soup in silence, letting Aunt Winnifred and the Don carry the conversation. Her stolen glances in the Don's direction provided no clue to his earlier behavior in the chapel.

It was he, I'm sure it was. One moment his arms held me, the next moment he was gone. In the chapel he was dressed as a bandito, now he reappears as a Don. Which is he—or is he both? Either way, he cannot be trusted. I am still his captive. Felicia touched her fingertip to her heart-shaped lips, still sensing the pressure of his mouth against hers, the pounding in his chest against her . . .

"Senorita Felicia—"

Felicia looked up dreamily as that same deep voice called her back from the sweet memory of the morning to the moment at hand.

"Senorita, I—"

The Don was about to address her when they were distracted by the appearance of the old Indian at the dining room archway.

Don Andres stood up. His eyes, like hard flint, met those of the expressionless old man head on.

"They have crossed the bridge," the old Indian said tonelessly. Then he turned and slipped away as stealthily as he had entered.

"Pardon me, ladies. It appears we will have visitors shortly. I would appreciate it if you would wait in your room. You will be safer there." With that, he put down his napkin and strode purposefully from the room.

Felicia and her aunt rose immediately and, without saying a word, hurried to the northern wing of the sprawling hacienda.

Once safely behind closed doors, Felicia whispered, "This place grows more mysterious by the minute. Did you see the fearful look in the majordomo's eyes as we passed him in the hall?"

"Life on this frontier isn't fun and games,

Felicia. We are squarely in the middle of a war."

A minute later Fawn Eyes appeared at their bedroom door with a tray containing their unfinished food.

"Thank you, Fawn Eyes. Do you know who is riding up to the rancho?"

"Yes, Senorita. Californios. They are driving cattle into the mountains to hide them from the American army. They want the Don to give them his horses and cattle."

"Will he do it, Fawn Eyes?"

"I do not know, Senorita."

"Please, go and listen. When they have gone, come tell us what happened."

The child nodded obediently and left.

Felicia picked up her cape and handcase, whispering excitedly, "Hurry, Aunt Winn, it is time. Get your things and follow me."

"What about our trunks, Felicia?" Then Aunt Winn's eyes scanned the room. "They're gone!"

"No matter. We can't carry them anyway, Aunt Winn. Come on. We may have only a few minutes' head start."

The two hurried on tiptoes down the tiled arcade to the back entrance of the rancho. The rustle of taffeta and the padding of soft leather were easily camouflaged by the arrival of pounding hoofbeats and loud voices. Felicia's fleeting guess was that about two dozen riders were fast approaching.

Once safely at the back door, Felicia stepped out and peeked around the patio wall. The buckboard was still there and no one was in sight. She motioned to Aunt Winn and the two darted across the rain-dampened grass to the wagon.

A tarpaulin covered the cargo bed. Felicia did not take time to loosen the rope and pull back the cover. Instead, she tossed their cases under the seat, then ran and untied the horse while Aunt Winn climbed aboard. A minute later the pair was on its way down the north trail, galloping away from Rancho del Dios, away from their captor!

Felicia allowed the mare to slow to a trot once they had put a quarter-hour and the rain-swollen creek between them and their prison on the hilltop. They rode below leaded skies that grew more threatening as the minutes wore on.

"If it starts to pour, we can take shelter in that stand of trees about a mile ahead of us," Felicia said, giving the horse a brisk slap of the reins.

"How do you know we're going in the right direction?" Aunt Winn inquired, drawing her windblown cape more closely around her and giving her bonnet ribbon a tightening tug against the weather.

"I *don't* know. For all I know, Rancho El Camino may be south of Rancho del Dios. We took the only undetected route away from Santiago's rancho available to us. This trail is well-traveled, so it must lead somewhere. Anywhere is better than staying cooped up in prison."

Aunt Winn threw back her head and laughed. "You may look like your mother, but you are definitely your father's daughter—an adventurer at heart. You know that we're laying a perfect set of tracks?"

Felicia nodded affirmatively as she leaned forward and squinted. "I think there's a fork in the road ahead." A raindrop splattered on the tip of her upturned nose.

"Yes, I see it. One fork heads off to the east. Do you recognize any landmarks from your childhood, Felicia?"

"I have no idea where we are." Felicia was completely exasperated.

Then the floodgates of heaven swung open wide and the deluge began.

"The decision's made," Felicia called out, spurring the dappled mare on. "We're staying to the main trail. We'll cut over to those trees ahead. Pray that the rain washes our traces into oblivion."

Even under the oaks the rain continued to dampen the escapees through the holes in their leafy umbrella.

"We could crowd under the wagon," suggested Aunt Winn.

"Better yet," Felicia suggested, "let's get under the tarpaulin."

They reached over the back of the seat and drew back the edge of the heavy oilskin.

"Fawn Eyes!" Felicia exclaimed. "What are you doing among those trunks?"

"Felicia, those are our trunks. Don Andres *was* planning to take us to Rancho El Camino!"

Felicia hesitated, her head swirling with conflicting emotions. She looked questioningly at Fawn Eyes.

"After lunch," the young girl acknowledged. "The Don said I could go along and be the Senorita's maid until the wedding—just as he promised."

What could be his purpose in perpetrating this marriage lie?

"How...how did you get into the wagon?" Felicia managed to stammer.

"The best listening place is behind the patio wall. From there, I could hear the Don speaking to the Californios. That is when I saw you run across the grass to the carreta. I followed and climbed on the back as it pulled away. I wiggled under the cover to hide."

"A stowaway," laughed Aunt Winnifred.

"Now *we* are the kidnappers," Felicia giggled.

"Are we going to Rancho El Camino?" Fawn Eyes asked innocently.

"I hope so," smiled Felicia, "if we can find the way. Would you know how to get there, Fawn Eyes?"

"Yes, Senorita. I have been there many times to see my cousin. Do you want me to show you the way?"

"Oh, yes. Please." Felicia took the hand of the young Indian girl and together they trudged through the wet leaves to the edge of the tree line.

Fawn Eyes pointed. "See the road that goes toward the morning sunrise? That is the one you must take. It crosses the creek two more times before it ends at Rancho El Camino."

The two ran back to the carreta. "We're heading back to the fork in the road, Aunt Winn. You and Fawn Eyes tuck yourselves under the oilcloth and pray—pray that the rain keeps falling."

Moments later Felicia had them back on the trail facing eastward. Heavy rain drenched her; flying mud pelted her. The wind blew into Felicia's face, stinging until her cheeks turned a deep rose color. But nothing could dampen Felicia's joy. She would be home at

Rancho El Camino within the hour!

She gave Greystone full rein across the open meadows and pulled her in to conserve her energy on sections of the trail where the one-wagon caravan was safely hidden from searching eyes by clumps of trees or protective rock outcroppings.

Felicia guided the carreta across the second rain-swollen creek and was picking her way through heavily wooded terrain when something a few yards ahead suddenly caught her attention.

"A rockslide!" she announced disgustedly. Felicia brought cart and horse to a standstill in the middle of the narrow trail. There was no way to go around the pile of rocks and boulders.

"Did you say something about a rockslide?" asked Aunt Winn, poking her head out from underneath the tarpaulin.

Fawn Eyes peeked out, too, then exclaimed in a panicked tone, "Senorita, that's not a natural rockslide. That's the work of Indians!"

Felicia grabbed the reins and jerked them toward her. They would go back to the river and turn around.

"Don't bother, Felicia. Look." Aunt Winnifred's voice was somber, her gaze fixed on the trail ahead.

"They're behind us, too," whispered Fawn Eyes. "I hear them in the trees."

Felicia refused to give in without a fight. "Heads down and hold on," she whispered. "We're going to turn around and run down a couple of savages if we have to."

Felicia cracked the whip. The lathered mare bolted ahead into a 180-degree turn, nearly tipping over the cart when one wheel slid over the outer edge of the hillside trail. Once out of the quick turn and back on the trail, the carreta responded to the horse's pull. Felicia and her cargo charged out of the snare.

Suddenly three war-whooping Indians jumped out from behind trees several yards ahead of them, blocking their escape. Felicia cracked the whip again and hung on. One of the Indians grabbed Greystone's bridle, another leaped up on her back. The animal was brought to an abrupt, whinnying halt.

"What do you want?" ordered Felicia, more angry than frightened at the half-dressed natives.

"Whatever you have to eat, Senorita," responded the smooth-skinned young brave who had grabbed the bridle.

He flashed a knife and in a single swiftness cut the rope at the back corner of the cart. He threw back the tarpaulin and laughed.

"Look at this! Fawn Eyes and a skinny old lady hiding among the cases. Are you afraid of us?" He laughed again, mockingly.

Fawn Eyes sat up straight. Felicia noticed for the first time how like a waif the young girl appeared with her stringy hair and simple dress.

Dress? How selfish I have been! The child has no wrap. No wonder she looks like a drowned rat. She must be freezing!

"You shame our people, Running Coyote. Chief Cota will hear of your cowardice."

Felicia held her breath, watching Running Coyote's reaction to the child's tongue-lashing.

He paid little heed to Fawn Eyes' words. "Open

the trunks, little one. Pull out the fine wine. Chief Cota will be the first to drink to our good fortune and rich booty.''

Fawn Eyes fumbled with the latch on the first trunk. Impatient, the young brave pushed the young girl aside and broke open the lock with a swipe of his knife blade.

Minutes later the buckboard was a mass of vivid colors—Felicia's beautiful red satin ball gown, velvet slips, taffeta morning coats. Some of her finest garments were strewn over the back of the carreta, as was Aunt Winnifred's pink, sheered tea dress and her new redingote, made of white India muslin, lined with pale-blue silk.

Finally, after every case had been opened and ransacked, Running Coyote's companions mounted and were about to ride off empty-handed.

''Wait!'' Running Coyote suggested, ''We need wine and food. Surely the Don that Fawn Eyes works for will trade the beautiful Senorita for many bottles of wine and much red meat.''

His companions shook their heads. The lead rider kicked his horse's belly with a moccasined heel and rode off. The other young braves followed.

''They run like scared squaws,'' the brave scoffed.

''They know that Don Andres Santiago has been good to our people. Many Luisenos work on the rancho,'' said Fawn Eyes.

''Who are to to tell me, little one? I worked for the Don cleaning stables while you were still a papoose. I even went to school on the rancho until. . .''

"Until when?" Felicia interrupted.

The young brave looked at Felicia, seemingly confused for a moment. Then he smiled. "It doesn't matter to you. All you want to do is keep me here, hoping the Don will ride up and save you again. Even the Don knows better than to defy the gods a second time."

A second time?

Suddenly Running Coyote rode his horse close to where Felicia was sitting on the buckboard. He made a quick grab for her, attempting to pull her over onto the back of his well-trained horse.

"I didn't need saving the first time and I certainly don't need saving a second!" Felicia shouted with scalding fury.

Running Coyote fought to keep his balance and to gain a firm hold on Felicia. She squirmed wildly, managing to get one good kick into the side of the horse's belly with the pointed toe of her leather shoe.

Unnerved, the skittish mount sidestepped, unsettling Running Coyote.

The Indian's muscles tightened as he attempted to regain control of his stallion without loosening his grip around Felicia's waist. Felicia twisted around and swung at Running Coyote's face, clawing at him with her long fingernails.

He dodged, but too late. A streak of blood trickled down his painted face. Shock yielded to fury, and curses spewed from his mouth.

He let out a blood-curdling cry and spurred his nervous horse—just as Fawn Eyes jumped from the edge of the wagon into the horse's path.

The stallion reared straight up. His nostrils flared; his hooves beat the air.

In the next split second Running Coyote dropped Felicia into a heap on the ground and whipped his mount on the flank.

Stunned, Felicia looked up in time to see the horse's hoof coming down toward her head. She felt excruciating pain and then there was nothing.

7

*T*he air was filled with the aroma of his pipe tobacco. Felicia didn't have to open her eyes to know that her beloved father was within her arm's reach. *At last, journey's end.*

She smiled inwardly, absorbing the warmth of true contentment. Unconcerned that she was too weak to open her eyes, Felicia drifted peacefully away.

Sometime later she floated back to consciousness, eagerly seeking the security of that same aroma. It wasn't there!

Fear coursed through her. She struggled desperately to wake up. *Father, come back! I worked so hard to reach you in time. Where are you?*

Then, too exhausted to fight the heavy web of blackness a moment longer, Felicia gave in and fitfully drifted out of reach of those keeping a constant vigil at her bedside.

The tall-case clock in the entry hall struck each hour, one after the other, day after day. Felicia did not respond to the chiming of her treasured childhood companion until midway through the ninth day of her unconsciousness.

As she awakened, she counted three chimes, each ringing clearly in her ears. Felicia opened her eyes slowly. It was daylight. The fuzzy objects in the room exuded an aura of the familiar, but what anything was eluded her. Gradually her vision sharpened and the windows, draperies, and Duncan Phyfe chest all came into sharp focus. She was in her own room at Rancho El Camino!

Praise God! Her heart sang with relief.

The afternoon sun streamed through the windows. She was alone in the bedroom, but sensed that it was only for the moment. Felicia didn't mind; she needed time to gather her wits.

Her last remembered moments rushed to the forefront of her mind—the rockslide, the Indians darting out from behind the trees, Running Coyote's strong arm around her waist, and her anger at his audacity. Imagine, wanting to barter her for a case of wine and a side of beef!

Suddenly the picture of Fawn Eyes loomed before her, just as the Indian child had loomed up in front of the horse, startling him, causing him to rear.

Felicia sat up and touched her forehead. She felt the bandage that wound around her head. Then terror washed over her as she relived the instant that the horse's hoof struck its blow; she felt once again the spike of pain that had crushed her consciousness.

Felicia grabbed the sides of her head and winced. Gradually the pain lessened and left her. She fell back on her pillow, completely spent.

Fawn Eyes risked her life to save mine. That beast could have trampled her to death! Then she thought, *I don't know that he didn't! I don't know what happened after I blacked out or even how I got here!*

"Welcome home, Felicia Maria."

Don Juan Las Flores ducked through the doorway, his broad shoulders scraping the sides of the opening. The sea-blue sparkle of his eyes brightened the whole room. Even as she called his name he was limping toward her. A moment later she was smothered against his chest. The aroma of his pipe tobacco filled her nostrils, and his beard, grown completely white with time, scratched color into her pale cheeks.

"Oh, Father, thank God, our prayers are answered. You are alive!"

Gently he laid her back on the pillow. "That I am, Daughter. And I am so thankful that you are safely here that I haven't the heart to scold you for the lunacy you and your doting aunt displayed by making the insane journey from Boston."

"On the contrary, Father," Felicia countered,

"I'm only sorry that it took a desperate situation to give me the courage to come. I should have returned home following graduation. The twins will not be dissuaded once they've finished their schooling. They've made that very clear. We all want very much to be together, here with you."

Felicia pressed on, realizing that her father was listening to her with the attentiveness that one adult gives another.

"What good are we to each other as a family if we spend our lives a continent apart? The moment I stepped on the veranda at Rancho Rincon del Diablo, I knew my roots lay deep in rancho soil. I meant it when I told Aunt Winnifred that I was in California to stay. And from what little I've seen of rancho life, teachers are greatly needed on the Frontier."

"We'll deal later with the weighty subject of where you'll be living permanently. Right now I want to get a good look at you. Dear God, how blessed I am to have your dear mother's beauty alive in this house once again!"

Felicia watched as his face began to cloud over. Then, as if caught with his guard down, the Don quickly cleared his throat and said lightly, "Nine days of you lying unconscious is enough to last a lifetime. It's time for a fiesta. We'll celebrate your eye-opening!"

Felicia smiled up at him adoringly.

The Don settled down on a chair close to her bed and took his daughter's slender hand in the palm of his own large, gnarled one, still covered with a mat of red hair.

"Father, tell me, is Fawn Eyes all right? I owe her my life."

"Yes, Dear, she escaped the horse's flailing completely by darting away quicker than a trout dodging a shadow from above. However, she was unconsolable when you couldn't be awakened. She was certain that you had been dashed to death by Running Coyote's mount."

"That poor child..."

"Fortunately, Winnifred was able to calm her by showing her how to feel your pulse. Both were relieved to find that you had one."

"I'd forgotten that Aunt Winn was once a nurse."

"Aunt Winn? Where's your respect? Is this the result of allowing women the privilege of higher education?"

Felicia giggled. "You know how I adore Aunt Winnifred, Father. I call her Aunt Winn with her permission. She says it makes her feel younger."

Then, rubbing her hand against her father's well-trimmed beard, she asked seriously, "Tell me truthfully. Are you sure you're fully recovered from the injuries that nearly took your life?"

"I am fine, truly, except for a wobble that is corrected by this fancy cane." He held up the gold-headed walking stick for Felicia to see. "I don't mind carrying it. It gives me an air of dignity, don't you agree?"

"That it does, Father, that it does."

Felicia lay back and closed her eyes. She rested for a moment before venturing on her new course. Finally she asked, "Tell me why the Indians attacked and how we can keep them from raiding the rancho again."

Don Juan Las Flores chuckled and shook his head. "I send a dainty little girl east to learn etiquette and art history. Who returns? A beautiful, grown woman who would rather talk business to me than to ask what handsome, rich suitor has paced the parlor daily since—"

Felicia pushed herself up on one elbow. "The war is over, isn't it?" Her dark eyes sparkled, awaiting confirmation.

Her father nodded slowly. "What makes you think that, Felicia? I have not said anything that would—"

"He would only be here if the United States was victorious in battle. How did he know where to find me?" Felicia felt a warm glow flow through her body.

"What are you babbling about, my darling daughter? The war is not over—quite yet. However, Pico was routed by the U.S. Army in San Pascual Valley on the sixth. Three days later our boys were backed up Mule Hill—a perilous situation indeed. Kit Carson and two others bellied past the enemy, then separated to better their chances. All three managed to reach San Diego, busting into Bandini's fancy-dress ball to get the news to Stockton—I would have loved to see that sight! Anyway, when order was restored, Stockton sent a detachment of 100 tars and eighty Marines marching to the rescue."

"Praise the Lord," Felicia sighed.

"We believe we've seen the end to resistance in San Diego. All Mexican flags have disappeared, and rumor has it that the Bandini sisters are sewing an American flag bearing twenty-six stars."

"Wha . . . what day is this? I can't believe that I slept through the Battle of San Pascual! Is

Captain Crane all right? He can't have been too badly injured if he is able to pace—"

The Don broke in with a hearty laugh. Still, there were tears in his eyes. "I've prayed for the moment you would awaken and speak to me. Now, after only five minutes, you have completely befuddled my aging brain with your nonsensical chatter. Let's take your questions one at a time, shall we?"

Felicia nodded happily. It seemed as though she had never been away.

"First, Felicia dear, today is Monday, the thirteenth of December."

"It is? I've missed so much. Tell me everything, beginning with Captain Crane. Do you like him, Father?"

"Captain Crane?" The Don's brow wrinkled questioningly. "I've never heard of the man, Dear."

Felicia's long lashes blinked unbelievingly at him.

"Are 'he' and Captain Crane one and the same?"

Felicia nodded yes.

"Where did you meet this Captain Crane, Felicia? And why should he have trouble finding you?"

Felicia felt an unwelcome blush creep into her cheeks. "He's...he's a Captain in the First Dragoons," she stammered. "I'm sure Aunt Winn has told you the details of our journey, including those of the night we spent under the protection of the U.S. Army."

"She did indeed. So that's when this Captain Crane made a play for my daughter, is it? I can't fault him for his good taste. He asked permission to come courting once the First Dragoons polished off the enemy. Right?"

"You make him sound...common," Felicia responded defensively. Then her hurt turned to annoyance.

"He's not common at all, Father." Her cheeks burned with the secret remembrance of their tender good-bye, witnessed only by the harvest moon.

The Don raised his palm as if taking an oath. "I'm sorry, Felicia. I have no right to prejudge the captain. Our men in blue have done the nation proud. We owe each one a great debt. Undoubtedly Crane is a gentleman of the finest reputation or you would not have given him the time of day. Still, he has not presented himself here at the rancho or at our city residence above the Presidio since the First Dragoons marched into San Diego."

"How do you know?" Felicia asked uncertainly.

"Alfredo, my majordomo, rode out this morning with the week's mail and news of the troops' arrival in San Diego. He would have advised me had there been an inquiry concerning Senorita Las Flores."

Felicia bit her lip and turned her head away from her father. In a voice laced with despair she confessed, "He'll never find me, even if he chooses to call on me. I told him my name was Felicia Worthington."

The room hung in heavy silence. Finally the Don asked in a low, searching tone, "Is Captain Crane *very* special to you, my dear Felicia?"

"Don't ask me, Father. I am too humiliated now to know the answer to that question myself."

"Then forget him, my child," the Don commended.

Felicia tightened her quivering jaw in a fruitless effort to stem the welling tears.

"Allow this flesh wound to heal quickly before it festers beyond common sense," he advised, his tone markedly softer.

Felicia swallowed hard. Logic told her that her father was right.

She closed her eyes and envisioned herself gathering her feelings for the handsome captain into the image of her mother's lace handkerchief. She sealed it mentally with an errant tear or two, then tucked it away in a corner of her anguished heart.

Give me peace, Lord. Keep me mindful of Romans 8:28: "All things work together for good to them that love God."

"It's time for a fresh subject," she heard her father say. "What is your next question, Felicia dear?"

Felicia took a deep breath. After a moment she turned toward her father and asked in a voice void of enthusiasm, "I am curious to learn why Alfredo is staying in the Presidio house in the city."

"I've kept a full staff there for the last month. Frankly, there's been some trouble."

"From whom?"

"Disgruntled Indians, Mexican sympathizers."

"What kind of trouble?"

"Kidnappings, raids, isolated killings. There was even a poisoning reported—an Indian cook salted his master's dinner with the extract of a deadly root.

"The atmosphere in San Diego in the days prior to Kearny's victory was volatile at best. I had no intention of allowing you to enter the city, let alone attempt to cross enemy lines north of the pueblo."

The Don leaned back in his chair and crossed his arms.

Felicia's mind raced. Her father had faked the ambush! Don Andres had abducted her upon her father's orders, to keep them from falling into the clutches of the enemy. Even Running Coyote knew Santiago had saved her—but from what? Felicia felt a knot of anger begin to tighten in the pit of her stomach.

"Your Don Santiago got a bit carried away, Father. He frightened Aunt Winn and me out of our wits, dragging us off like criminals. He never did explain that it was all an act."

The Don grinned proudly. "I heard that he was quite convincing."

Felicia bolted upright, her dark eyes flashing. "I fail to see the humor. I don't think a Don's daughter should be made to play the role of a fool!"

The color drained from the Don's face. At once Felicia knew that she had overstepped her bounds.

His tone controlled the fire in his words. "The part you played convinced the birds listening in the trees. Sometimes, Felicia, it is better to act the fool than to be one."

Felicia lay back down and lowered her eyes. It was a standoff.

Neither spoke until she asked, "How did you know I was on that particular stage, or for that matter, that I was on my way to California?"

"Alfredo told me of his letter to you, once he realized that I was truly on the mend. I could not be angry with him for writing you. Alfredo feared that the rancho would fall into enemy hands should I die without an heir on the property. And that's exactly what would have happened.

"It then became a matter of watching for each cross-country stage traveling the San Pascual Valley route. There are not many. You were on the second possible one."

The San Pascual Valley route? How could he know who was on the second stage? No one stopped us. The only living soul we met prior to the ambush was the old Indian at the abandoned Rancho Rincon del Diablo.

Felicia scowled. *The old Indian. . . the old Indian. Something about that old man.*

Felicia looked her father directly in the eyes. "I knew I had seen Don Santiago's old stable hand somewhere—somewhere before that frightening moment he sneaked up behind us with a hatchet!"

The puzzle pieces fell into place.

"Now I know why the abandoned rancho was swept clean and there were plump chickens ready for plucking. Don Andres' old Indian was camped at Rancho Rincon del Diablo, waiting for us to arrive."

It was then that Felicia was reminded of Don Andres' words: "Tonight you will dine on more than roast chicken and winter squash."

Felicia continued to pick up the odd pieces.

"After providing breakfast the old Indian, by riding hard, still had time to reach Don Andres and alert him of our presence in the neighborhood. The Don then set out to intersect our stage before it reached enemy-held territory."

Her father acknowledged her cleverness with a sober nod.

Felicia reached up and slipped her arms

around her father's neck. "I love you so much. Thank you for thinking me worthy of such life-saving heroics."

"I'm not the only one who values your life, Felicia. Don Andres saved your life a second time when he chased after you and found you lying unconscious on the trail. He was the one who rushed you to Rancho El Camino."

"Don Andres brought me here?"

"He did. You can't imagine how shocked he was when he discovered that you had stolen away from his rancho. You were his responsibility. He knew you had no comprehension of the dangers that lurked in your path."

"Running Coyote, for one."

The Don measured his tone once again when he uttered the words: "Running Coyote was hunted down and shot before the moon crested the eastern peaks."

Don Andres—arrogant kidnapper, bandit, and now murderer.

A shiver ran down Felicia's spine. "Thank heaven the play-acting is over. Worse than being bartered for beef is to be sold as a bride!"

Don Juan took both of Felicia's hands into his and held them tightly. His face appeared suddenly drawn and tired-looking. His eyes were washed out to a faded blue.

"Felicia," he choked, "that part was not play-acting. You are to be Don Andres' bride. I've given my word—as a Don."

8

" " 97...98...99...100. Look
● ● ● how my hair shines, Fawn
Eyes! Brushing is good for your hair. It gives life
and radiance."

The young Indian girl stepped back and watched
as Felicia swished her thick, raven-black hair
to and fro. The warming, midmorning light
streaming through the windows caught the long
tendrils and laid a rich luster on the natural curls
cascading over Felicia's narrow shoulders and

down the back of her peach-colored cashmere morning dress.

"Your hair is the most gorgeous I've ever seen, Senorita," Fawn Eyes said sincerely.

Felicia smiled and put her hand on the young girl's arm. "Here, Fawn Eyes, sit down in front of the vanity mirror. Let me show you how to brush your hair the way I learned from a famous hairdresser in Boston."

"Oh, no, Senorita, I couldn't!"

Felicia slipped her arm around Fawn Eyes' slender waist and coaxed the reluctant girl toward the velvet-cushioned stool. "It is my wish," she said lightly. Then, picking up her treasured, inlaid hairbrush, Felicia began the arduous task of unsnarling her little maid's long, stringy hair.

The longer Felicia worked, the more relaxed Fawn Eyes became. Finally Felicia felt comfortable asking, "Why is it that you do not brush your own hair as beautifully as you brush mine?"

Fawn Eyes responded simply, "I do not have a brush, Senorita. Someday, maybe..."

Astonished, Felicia met the child's gaze in the large beveled mirror. Fawn Eyes was not teasing.

Felicia composed her thoughts, as though she were back in the classroom preparing to make an important point. "Fawn Eyes," she asked softly, "where did you learn to speak English?"

"In the schoolhouse on the rancho."

"Rancho del Dios?"

"*Si*. My mother speaks English also. She learned from the *padre* at the mission. Her family lived there until forced to leave."

"Forced?"

The girl shrugged her thin shoulders. "You know, when Mexico closed the California missions, the Indians had to find new homes. Our family was most lucky, I am told. My mother moved to Don Santiago's Rancho del Dios, where I was born."

"Are you a Christian, Fawn Eyes?"

"Every morning my mother covers her head with a *mantilla* and goes to the chapel to pray."

Felicia stopped brushing and turned Fawn Eyes to face her. She got down on one knee to meet the girl at eye level. She took Fawn Eyes' tiny brown hands into her own.

"Do you—yourself—believe in Jesus Christ, Fawn Eyes?"

"I . . . I don't know much about Jesus. There's a Holy Book in the chapel that tells about Him, but we are not allowed to touch it. I did look close once and I found that I could read some of the words."

Felicia remembered the fragile beauty of that precious, gold-leafed volume, too delicate to be handled, even by the padre himself.

Wouldn't it be wonderful if every child could have his or her own clothbound Testament? Each could learn to read and to know Jesus Christ—at the same time.

"Would you like to know more about Jesus and how you may have everlasting life in heaven by believing in Him?"

"Yes, I think so. My mother says that the best way to know God is to talk to Him." Then she added, "My mother says that she talks to God in her prayers. She taught me the Lord's Prayer. Sometimes I remember to say it before I fall asleep.''

''Sometimes I talk to God during the day too, Fawn Eyes. I make up my own prayers. I try to remember to thank Him for all the good things that happen, as well as asking Him to get me out of trouble—I seem to get into plenty of that.''

Fawn Eyes looked down at the floor, drawing a circle with her well-worn shoe. ''Once,'' she confessed to Felicia, ''I asked Jesus to bring me a doll for Christmas, but He didn't do it.''

Felicia felt a lump rise in her throat for the poor waif. ''God does work miracles, Fawn Eyes, but He also works through people, in His own time. He knows what is best for each of us.''

Felicia picked up the heirloom she had been cradling in her lap. ''I want you to have this brush, Fawn Eyes. It is my 'thank you' gift for saving my life on the trail. I will never forget the sacrifice you were willing to make for me.''

Fawn Eyes looked up at Felicia with her large, doe-brown eyes. ''I could not take such a gift,'' she responded halfheartedly. ''It is a treasure from your mother. Besides, I was only obeying my master's orders—to stay with you and protect you until your wedding.''

Felicia cringed. Then she quickly pressed the brush into the girl's hand. ''I know Don Andres did not expect you to carry his command as far as you did. Nevertheless, my own mother, were she here, would approve of what I am doing. She would say that this is an example of God working through another person. First, He used you to save my life. Secondly, He is using me to provide you with something that will be very useful to you."

Fawn Eyes held the brush tenderly, examining it with pride.

"Each time you use it, remember the blessing that goes with it. Faith in Jesus Christ gives new life and an inner radiance that is everlasting."

"Thank you. I will remember. But Senorita, would you tell the housekeeper that you have given me your hairbrush? Otherwise she will think I have stolen it."

"Of course, I will speak to her immed—"

"Felicia, you have a guest waiting," interrupted Aunt Winn, appearing suddenly at the bedroom door.

"I'm glad you're back, Aunt Winn. Did you have any luck with my father?" she asked hopefully.

"Well, yes...and no."

"What do you mean 'yes and no'?"

"The explanation is rather complicated," she began, a wrinkle crossing her brow.

Then, realizing the reason for Aunt Winn's hesitancy, Felicia quickly excused Fawn Eyes to go and show off her new possession.

"I mean that your father is excitedly planning a welcome-home fiesta for this Saturday. The neighboring Dons and their families are invited. And he is pleased that you feel well enough to accept Juan Bandini's invitation to attend a Christmas week dinner-dance at their home in the city."

"It sounds wonderful. I'm delighted that my father will accompany us. I don't believe he has done much socializing since my mother died."

Then Felicia's manner sobered. "That was the 'yes' part," she said reservedly. "Now tell me the 'no' part, Aunt Winn."

"Ah...no, he hasn't changed his mind. You will marry Don Andres on the first day of the New Year."

"That's less than three weeks away! Why doesn't he put me out of my misery and hold the ceremony today? It makes a mockery of my social 'coming out.' "

"Felicia! Stop feeling sorry for yourself this instant! Your father is not allowing you 'the social season' to prolong your distress. Don't you see? He wants and needs the pride of introducing his eldest daughter to San Diego's society. Remember, he has sacrificed too. Although separated from your father, you three girls have had each other during the last six years. He has had no one. Don Juan is thrilled that you are here, and he is not anxious to have you marry and leave the rancho, though he will never tell you so himself."

"Why not? He knows that I do not want to marry the barbarian he has chosen for me!"

"Have you taken leave of your senses, girl? Any fool can see that your father regrets his action. But once a Don has given his word..."

"I'm the one making the vow at the marriage altar, not my father! I am not chattel, to be given or sold on another's whim. I want to choose my own husband, in my own time—to marry only for love, not to honor a business contract!"

"Felicia, have you given a moment's consideration as to why your father gave his word in the first place?"

"No...I..."

"Well, I have," she snapped, "and the options I come up with are not pleasant ones. I suggest that we expend our energy pursuing that mystery before we waste any more effort feeling frustrated over your state of affairs."

"But, Aunt Winn..."

"Like it or not, Felicia, the Dons are the law of the land in California, and will continue to be so until the United States government establishes a uniform, enforceable government in the West."

"That's more like three years than three weeks away!"

"I think you're beginning to see my point, Dear."

There had to be a way... Felicia paced the bedroom floor. She was caged and she knew it.

Finally Felicia conceded. "You're right, Aunt Winn. It appears that Don Andres holds the key to a great many mysteries, and I've done my best to alienate myself from him and his confidence."

The clock chimed.

Aunt Winn stood up and motioned to her niece. "Let's get you dressed."

While she helped Felicia slip into her new satin-lined, mint-green walking dress she said, "Remember, Felicia, it is quicker to catch a fly with honey than with flypaper."

"Your advice is well-taken, Aunt Winn," Felicia smiled.

"Good. Here's some more. Don Andres is talking with your father while he waits for you. From what I overheard as I left, neither man is in a mood to put up with the slightest procrastination or the excuse of a faint heart, especially after your miraculous recovery of the past two days."

"Has something happened?"

"Yes, but I don't know what it is. I believe I heard the word 'massacre' used."

"It was probably *masquerade*."

"No, I don't think so. My advice is *don't press*. Something terrible is troubling both of them."

"I understand. Thank you."

"Oh, Felicia, I almost forgot. There is something else. It has to do with your Captain Crane."

"What is it? Tell me," Felicia pleaded. She stopped fluffing her honeycombed crinoline petticoat and turned her full attention to her aunt.

"You awakened on the afternoon of the thirteenth?"

"Yes, yes. Go on."

"Your father told you that Captain Crane had not called at the Presidio house?"

"Correct. Alfredo rode out from the city on that very morning with supplies and the week's mail. He made no mention to my father of any gentleman caller inquiring..."

Aunt Winn's gold-flecked eyes darted excitedly. "Felicia, our troops, exhausted, half-naked, and hauling many injuried on makeshift stretchers, did not reach San Diego until December 12. They arrived amid torrents of rain and were taken immediately to the abandoned Mexican garrison—a wretched, dirty hole that had to be made livable."

Felicia tried not to dwell on the picture of filth and squalor that greeted her hero, her secret love. Instead she reached for perhaps her last ray of hope. "Which means...?" she questioned with anticipation.

"Which means, my darling niece, that in all fairness Captain Crane hasn't had time to seek you out."

"And today is only the sixteenth," Felicia reflected aloud.

Aunt Winn smiled knowingly. With a twinkle in her eyes she tied the bow on her surprise package. "Certainly, Felicia, the Captain cannot be faulted if he doesn't consider his own social life until, say...Christmas week."

Felicia's mouth curved into a bright smile that soon had her dark eyes dancing. The Christmas week dinner-dance at the Bandinis'! She could almost smell the mountain-fresh evergreens decorating the dining room and hear the enchanting strains of that new music sweeping the country—the waltz—as it wafted romantically from the adjoining ballroom.

She moved toward the mirror as if in a trance. Suddenly the mint-green of her long-sleeved walking dress was transformed into a rich, Christmas-red ball gown. The rows of black lace that formed a bodice-length V, starting at the shoulders of her high-necklined dress and extending to a deep-pointed waist, became a wide, edge-of-the-shoulder flounce of Brussels lace, setting off the softness of her alabaster skin. She imagined a dance card in her lace-gloved hand —with only one name neatly written across its face.

Felicia grabbed her Aunt and began twirling her around the room. "You're right!" she exclaimed. "There is still time for Father to meet Captain Crane—there is still time for him to change his mind!"

Felicia twirled around one more time, then spun free. She heard the hall clock chime again. Quickly she picked up her mint-green, fringed silk scarf and matching parasol.

Felicia, her cheeks the color of dew-fresh pink rosebuds and her dark eyes still sparkling, hummed a lilting waltz as she hurried toward the library to keep her appointment with Don Andres Santiago.

9

*D*on Andres flicked a small stone into the water. He and Felicia watched, fascinated, as the ripples multiplied and widened until they kissed the edges of most of the lily pads in the fish pond. A frog croaked here, a cricket answered there. All the while Felicia wondered about the depth of the man standing next to her.

"And there you have life on the Frontier," scoffed Don Andres, leaning heavily on the split-rail fence bordering the pond. Still, there was an air of isolation about the tall, dark-skinned man.

"I do not see the analogy." Felicia tossed her head coquettishly. Then, adjusting her parasol against the noon sun, she asked lightly, "Could you explain?"

The Don did not seem to notice Felicia's animation. His gaze was still on the pond a few feet in front of them. His furrowed brow told her that he was taking her question far more seriously than she had intended.

When he finally replied, his response was unhurried. "The Dons have so much power and so little control over it. While trying to improve life for some, we may inadvertently destroy it for others. Every action we take, no matter how small, is like tossing a pebble onto still waters. Ripples are inevitable. The broader they spread, the more difficult it is to control their course."

Heavy dialogue for a man a'courting, Felicia thought. *Well, then, so be it. There's also more than one brand of honey.*

The sun was hidden momentarily by the high, jagged outcropping of rock rising up behind them. A shadow sliced across the pool.

Felicia set aside her frivolous parasol and stepped closer to the fence. She rested her elbow on the railing and then shaded her deep, dark eyes with her hand. She waited, watching a passing school of goldfish nip playfully at one another.

Finally she broke the thoughtful silence between them with a simple, "For example?"

"The Indians, for one," was his readied reply. He continued to keep his eyes focused on the water as he elaborated.

"Father Junipero Serra suffered tremendous privations to establish twenty-one missions in California. By 1830 they were already beginning to decline, though the missions watched over the lives of more than 15,000 Christianized Indians, and their ranchos and farms were able to furnish enough food and goods to also support the dwindling Mexican military garrisons of California."

"Then why did the mission system collapse?" Felicia thought immediately of the ripple effect that the missions' failure had on the lives of Fawn Eyes, on the girl's mother, and even on Running Coyote.

"Mexico, torn by revolution and continuing political disorder, had enough to do in adjusting to its independence from Spain. Maintaining order over the vast territory of Spanish America became the responsibility of the Californios by default."

"What does this have to do with the Indians?"

Don Andres turned toward Felicia, his dark eyes scanning hers. It was as if he was noticing her for the first time since they had started their walk through Rancho El Camino's manicured gardens twenty minutes earlier.

"You are sincerely interested, aren't you, Felicia?"

"Yes," she replied, "I am. My roots are here. Still, it's more than that. There are so many needs here. The Lord has provided me with an education. I know how to meet some of those needs. The children on the rancho need a teacher..."

Then suddenly, *Those eyes! Those dark, liquid-*

*brown eyes! There is no question. Those were the eyes
hidden behind the bandito's mask! Why the disguise?
And why did he kiss me?*

Felicia's lips tingled in remembrance of his
touch. She lingered in that memory a long moment
before she realized that the Don had resumed his
monologue.

"...found themselves homeless, without food
or work. The Indians were angry at the Californios who had been deeded land, held in
trust for them by the Franciscan missionaries
in accordance with old Spanish law and custom."

Felicia caught enough of his explanation to judge
that her assessment of the situation to the Jenkinses had been correct. The progression of recent
events amounted to tossing sparks at an aging
powder keg.

"The Indians are now at least two revolutions
removed from enforceable 'old Spanish law,'"
Felicia commented.

Don Andres nodded. "They're running the range
on a short fuse. They want their land back.
Panic is fanning the situation and they're beginning to not care how they reclaim their birthright."

"The native Americans do have a point," Felicia
ventured cautiously.

"They do, but so do we. Fortunately, most tribal
councils recognize the contribution we have made
to their civilization: In learning our ways they have
improved their lifestyles and their health, and
many have been exposed to the rudiments of a
basic education. The majority of Dons have provided meaningful work and shelter to as many Indians as possible. Thousands are loyal, trust-
worthy..."

Suddenly the handsome Don's voice broke. He turned his back, but not before she saw his jaw tighten and a look of anguish cross his face.

Is it guilt that this Indian-murderer feels? wondered Felicia to herself. *He will not get my sympathy!*

She tried not to sound flippant. "Is it Running Coyote's death you mourn?"

He wheeled around, every muscle in his body taut. "I mourn the whole tribe—every man, woman, and child who will not live to see the new moon!" Anger filled his eyes; rage twisted his handsome face. "When is this bloodshed going to stop? I feel so powerless to do anything."

He buried his head in his hands. "They'll be tracked down like mad dogs—killed, cowering in the bushes. The Luiseno Indians are normally so docile... Why? What would drive them to...?"

Felicia's delicate hand flew to her throat. She grasped at the gold cross hanging around her neck.

"His whole tribe tracked down because you killed Running Coyote?"

He raised his head and stared at her—stunned. "*I* killed Running Coyote? Is that what you think?" His voice was steeled in disbelief.

"I heard—"

"Senorita, you heard wrong! Running Coyote was killed by other Indians who would not tolerate what he did to a respected Don's daughter. More frontier justice!"

"I didn't know—"

"Still, you judged." He seemed to condemn all of mankind with his terse statement.

Felicia grabbed the top railing to steady her quaking knees. First humiliation, then anger swept through her, choking the rising wave of rage. She bit her tongue lest she say what she was thinking.

Finally she spoke with measured control. "Then what are you talking about? Why do you fear more bloodshed?"

Don Andres looked at Felicia a long moment before allowing the muscles in his jaw to soften. Then he reached out and took one of her hands in his. Caressing her fingers gently, he replied hoarsely, "In a moment, my Senorita."

Felicia opened her mouth to protest. He touched his index finger to her lips for just an instant.

"Is that why you dislike me, Felicia?" he asked searchingly. "You believe me capable of murder?" The timbre of his voice bespoke the hurt mirrored in his dark eyes.

"I know that you are capable of kidnapping . . . though I've learned that my abduction was a ruse, planned by you and my father as part of—"

"Of what?" he pressed. "Please, go on."

"I have nothing more to say." Felicia spoke with finality.

It's clear, Felicia thought, noticing Don Andres' scowl, *that he is not accustomed to being defied—at least not by a woman.*

He sighed heavily. "I will answer your question. Perhaps then you will trust more and fear less those who try to protect you." Don Andres took her arm and they continued their walk along the garden path bordered by a row of brilliant scarlet-bracted poinsettias.

"Remember the day my friend, Juan Osuna, and his men came to my rancho, hoping to add my cattle to the herd that they were driving to Jose Serrano's rancho in Pauma Valley for safe-keeping?"

"Yes." Felicia wondered if the Don knew that she had chosen that moment of distraction for her quick escape from Rancho del Dios. Therefore she did not see or hear the riders' conversation.

"We have learned that following their defeat at San Pascual, several Californios went to Serrano's rancho, located in the shadow of Palomar Mountain, to rest. Osuna's youngest son was among them.

"A small tribe of Luiseno Indians live in the valley. Serrano, who understands a little of their language, overheard two women discussing a possible attack, and while he warned his houseguests, evidently none took the matter seriously. That day Serrano, his son, and his brother-in-law left the rancho to join the rest of their family in Pala.

"The inmates of the house were asleep when a knock came in the night. They knew better than to open the door, even though they recognized the voice of Luisenos Chief Cota. Still, they raised the bar. The Indians rushed in, seized their victims, and took them to Agua Caliente. There they were put on exhibition for the benefit of the Cupenos, Cahuillas, and Luiseno tribes."

By now the couple had stopped in the middle of the path under the shade of a towering sycamore. Felicia stood frozen in her tracks as Don Andres unraveled the gruesome tale to her.

"Several of us Dons understand that Cota had a last-minute change of heart, wanting to set the eleven captives free. Others opposed him, and we strongly feel that it was an American, Bill Marshall, majordomo at Warner's rancho, who added fuel to the fire by convincing the Indians to massacre the Californios. It is said that he told the Indians the American conquerors would be pleased.

"The moment Serrano returned to his rancho and discovered the spine-chilling truth of what he had overheard, he rushed to Agua Caliente and offered a ransom of cattle for the Californios' release. It was refused and his own life was threatened.

"It is unclear whether the captives were forced to stand and then were shot full of arrows or if they were lanced to death with spears heated in the fire. We do know that their lifeless forms were piled in a heap and the savage killers danced around them all night chanting their unholy rituals. Later their bodies were secretly buried."

Felicia closed her eyes as the tears welled up and overflowed, coursing down her now paled cheeks.

"Now you know why gloom hangs heavy over this day." His sense of loss seemed beyond tears. "Come, I will take you back to the hacienda." His voice sounded tired, his spirit spent.

Felicia's body ached with an inner pain that had no place of origin, no hope of relief as her thoughts churned. *Victors or victims? We are both—Indians, Californios, Americans. Is any frontier worth this price?*

Felicia suddenly understood the helpless feeling shared by those carving out a new frontier—the staid leaders of the Old World, the brave leaders of the New World, and the protectors of the Native World, each with differing views of law and order, promises and moral ethics.

"The choice is not 'Will we learn to live together?' or 'How soon?' The real question seems to be 'How much blood must flow before a living compromise is struck?' " reflected Felicia aloud.

Don Andres raised his arms and his voice to heaven as if asking God, "What can the Dons do to smother this range fire before it spreads across the West?"

Felicia reached out to him, putting her hand on his arm, even though she knew his grief was beyond comfort.

"Will you stay for lunch?" she asked softly, hoping he would.

"No, thank you. While talking to your father this morning, word reached me through Indian informers that young Osuna's body, along with another's, was turned over to an old Indian woman who had been a servant for their families. She is supposed to have buried their bodies apart from the others, then walked into San Diego with the sad news. She arrived only last night. I want to go now and be with the family during this time. If the rumor I hear is true, then I will offer to arrange a Christian burial for—"

"You are a Christian?"

"Yes," he replied matter-of-factly. A thin smile crossed his face, softening the seriousness of the last few minutes.

"It does not speak well for my witness of Christ

that you should be surprised. Whether evident or not, it is God's love, patience, and promise of life in paradise that sustains me during these mad days. We must be living in the end times!''

"How is it, then," Felicia blurted, "if you are a Christian, you follow the pagan practice of purchasing a wife?"

"Ah, the burr under the saddle finally surfaces, does it? 'If' I am a Christian? 'Pagan practice'? I haven't the inner strength to deal with our future now. However, I leave you with a question of my own. Ponder it carefully."

"What...what is it?" she asked him uncertainly.

"My darling Felicia, who chose Adam's wife for him?"

10

*A*unt Winn sat back from the breakfast table and folded her hands in
her lap to the rustle of her "Sunday best" taffeta
skirt.

"Don Andres has posed a provocative question,
Felicia. As you read aloud a moment ago from
Genesis 2, God decided that Adam needed a helpmate; and He brought the woman unto man. That
woman, chosen by the Father, was the perfect
choice for Adam."

"Your emphasis on 'chosen by the Father'—do you think that has special significance?" Felicia asked.

"Yes, I do. Every word in the Bible serves a purpose. The Bible is first a book of salvation. It is also, among other things, a book of instruction. Let's read what happened in the matter of wife selection, when God's example and teachings were not followed by His own people."

Aunt Winn thumbed her way through the early chapters of the Old Testament, stopping in Deuteronomy. "Read chapter seven, verses three and four, Dear. God gave strict instructions to His people regarding personal relationships with the conquered enemy: 'Neither shalt thou make marriages with them . . . for they will turn away thy son from following me, that they may serve other gods.'

"Now turn to the story of Noah's Ark and read how they disobeyed the Father and suffered for it."

An overcast December sky cast a pall over the well-lighted morning room as the two women concentrated on their daily devotion, selected on this morning of the home-coming fiesta by Felicia herself.

"I need to have an answer for Don Andres today, Aunt Winn." Felicia's tone reflected her troubled spirit which yearned for the right answer.

"I know, Dear," her aunt responded, her nimble hands quickly flipping back a few chapters in her well-worn Bible. Finally she stopped and ran her fingers down a page or two.

"Here it is, Felicia. Look at Genesis 6:2: 'The sons of God saw the daughters of men that they were fair, and they took them wives of all which they chose.'

"The emphasis here is on the word 'they.' 'They' defied God and did their own choosing. In verse five God saw that the wickedness of man was great. He repented that He had even made man, and vowed to destroy him. 'But Noah,' it says in verse eight, 'found grace in the eyes of the Lord.' Noah did according to all that God commanded him and in turn was saved in the flood which covered the earth.''

Aunt Winn closed her Bible and set it carefully on the table. She picked up her cup of coffee and took the first sip before Felicia raised her eyes from the gilt-edged page of the leather-covered Bible she had carried since childhood.

"I remember my Sunday school lessons. God blessed obedience, especially to parents, and repeatedly warned His people of the wages of sin. History bears out His admonitions repeatedly.''

"Then you remember in your Bible stories that the father, the head of the household, decided family matters, including who would marry whom. Oh, there were clever connivings and deceptions in the name of love and power, but sorrow was always the result of disobedience, just as it is today.

"God is not only a just God but He is a loving Father. Think of the many precious romances, blessed by God, laced among the Scriptures. The tender love story of Isaac and Rebekah, in Genesis 24, is the first that comes to mind.''

"There is little hope of romance in my life,'' Felicia sighed. She picked up a spoon and aimlessly stirred her cup of hot herb tea absent-mindedly.

She allowed her mind to wander a long moment among the clouds to that night of the harvest moon—a night sealed for all time by a tender kiss and the promise of love's tomorrow.

Felicia closed her eyes. She could feel his breath, so close that it brushed her cheeks. She felt the roughness of his handwoven serape against her alabaster skin. She tingled, remembering the possessiveness of his lips, hard against hers. She...

"Felicia! Are you all right?" Aunt Winn rose from her chair and rushed to her niece's side. "You're absolutely white. It's as if you've had a shock."

"What's going on here?" Don Juan strode into the room and fought his way around the heavy dining chairs to reach Felicia.

"Nothing. Really, it's nothing. I'm sure it's the excitement of today's fiesta," Felicia uttered unconvincingly. "I don't recall a party being held in my honor before."

"I believe that the 'nothing' is your insistence on keeping a tiny waistline at the expense of your health. Is that all you're having for breakfast, Felicia? A cup of tea? Let me order poached eggs..."

"No, Father. Aunt Winn and I had hot cereal and fruit before starting our morning devotion. I'm fine now. Truly I am."

Her father appraised her carefully. "Is something bothering you, Felicia?"

"If you'll excuse me, I'll go and speak with the housekeeper. I still have some loose ends to take care of in regard to today's menu."

Aunt Winn rose quickly and swished from the room.

Don Juan sat down and placed his long forearms openly on the table. The silver buttons on his jacket gleamed with fresh polish. He was honoring his soon-to-arrive guests by wearing his finest, most dazzling, silver-laden suit.

"What is it, Felicia? My sister's hasty departure tells me there *is* something on your mind. We haven't much time, so let's not beat about the bush, all right?"

Felicia studied her father's face. His concern was real, but the tight lines around his eyes marked a familiar impatience in his character. She decided to test her case carefully.

"I barely know Don Andres, whom you wish me to marry in less than three weeks, Father. I need to know something about him. It's only fair."

A slow smile crept across her father's ruddy face. The tension around his eyes seemed to disappear. "That is a reasonable request. I am only surprised that you haven't learned all there is to know in the length of time you've been here."

"Who is there to tell me? Don Andres is the most secretive man I've ever met. Certainly I would not ask any of the servants, nor would they know the answers to my questions."

He absentmindedly traced the hand-crocheted design of her mother's lace tablecloth with his ring finger.

"I hadn't given the matter a thought. I don't mean for you to be at a disadvantage or to be leery of Don Andres. What do you want to know, Felicia?"

Felicia treaded slowly, trying to sound calm.
"What is his background?"

"He's the nephew of a recent governor of
Mexico. His mother was Spanish, like yours.
His father was Mexican. The Don first came to
California as an army officer, distinguished
himself, and was elevated to the rank of captain. When the Mexican government began to
crumble, he left the service. He petitioned
for and was granted the rancho adjoining ours.
That's when I first met this remarkable young
man, who would now be in his early thirties."

"Remarkable?"

"Yes, especially in contrast to some of his
relatives, who are also Dons and wield their power
for greed and selfishness." He bristled and added,
"Under U.S. criminal law, they'd be strung
up!"

The tension lines were tightening once again
around her father's eyes. It was time to move
in another direction now. She would find out
what influence Don Andres' relatives had on
her father's life, if any, at another time...
soon.

"I noticed an abandoned schoolroom over at
Rancho del Dios. Why are classes no longer
held?"

"To begin at the beginning, I understand that
one of the padres from a 'closed' mission
wandered from rancho to rancho, as sort of a
circuit pastor, for a few years. When Don Andres acquired the land grant and began to build
a chapel in memory of his parents, the popular
padre came to live permanently at Rancho del
Dios. He spent his final years on this earth
supervising the construction of the chapel and

accumulating its furnishings. He acquired the chapel's priceless artifacts by 'various' methods.''

The Don cleared his throat and continued. ''Also, during that time, the padre established the school on the rancho and sought the help of an American teacher in San Diego, who shared books sent to her from the East. The children on the rancho attended classes daily for a couple of years.''

''It sounds perfect. What happened to spoil it? The padre's death?''

''Oh, no. An epidemic—smallpox, I think I heard it was. The superstitious Indians blamed their jealous gods and could not be coerced to send their children back to school. Finally Don Andres decided to stop trying to move a mountain single-handedly.''

''Perhaps when he has his own children to send...'' She stopped short, praying that the blush warming her cheeks now would disappear.

The tall-case clock chimed in the distance. Time was running out.

''Father, what hold does Don Andres have over you?''

Don Juan sat back with a start. ''Hold? What on earth do you mean, child?''

''How else could he force you to sell me to him? What was the purchase price?''

She watched the color drain from her father's temples. His form, already overpowering, suddenly filled the room, suffocating her.

''Felicia Maria! How dare you show such disrespect! It is my right, my *privilege,* to arrange a suitable marriage for you and your sisters. The moment I heard that you were on the way to California, I was reminded of your advancing age. I realized that the matter of your betrothal had to be one of my immediate priorities."

"Father, I am in no hurry to marry. Besides, I would prefer to choose my own husband."

"Your expensive modern education with its experimental values does not—I repeat, does *not*—alter the standards in this household or in those of ninety-nine percent of the rest of the world."

He paused long enough to catch his breath before continuing. "Could you be objective and were you experienced enough to weigh your future, you would find that there is not a man in California who holds a candle to Don Andres. Someday you will appreciate that fact."

Felicia did not intend to give in easily, even though her quivering voice betrayed her fearfulness. "Father, you married for love. That's the example I've wanted to follow."

His eyes narrowed. "Your mother's family arranged our marriage. It is true that I fell in love with your mother the moment we met. I courted her wildly. Once her father realized my serious intent, he forbade her to see anyone else. She and I were soon married."

Felicia was shattered. "Mother told me yours was a lovematch. She loved you with all her heart!"

"Of course she loved me. I know that. But she grew to love me *after* we were betrothed. Our love for each other multiplied with each day, with each year we shared together. True love is an experience that time together enriches."

"But what if Mother hadn't come to love you? You would have had a perfectly wretched marriage."

"That wasn't a possibility. Love is a learned behavior. With a full commitment to Jesus Christ, love for one another comes easily. I tried to love your mother as Christ loves the Church, as husbands are instructed in Ephesians 5. She, in turn, in Christian spirit, submitted herself to me in every way. Her duty soon became love on her part. We fully appreciated and respected each other." His voice choked up as he added, "She was the only *Dona* I have ever wanted in my life."

"Father," Felicia begged, reaching over and closing her hand over the top of his, "why did Don Andres boast that he had purchased me? He announced it loud and clear when he ambushed the stage."

"I answered that question before. That declaration to the world may have saved your life! At the very least, it was a requirement of your dowry."

"Dowry? What do you mean?"

"A dowry is common—you know that. In this case, I admit, the agreed-upon dowry is quite unusual."

"What is my dowry, Father?"

The Don freed his hand from hers and stood up. "That's where I draw the line, Felicia. The Don's business with me is private. You have more freedom than most young women of your station in this part of the country. Out of respect for your free-thinking ideas, resulting from the modern education I provided for you, I will not announce your engagement at today's fiesta. You are free to enjoy your social 'coming out' during the holiday festivities. In fact, I look forward to the role of escort for the brief season."

Felicia could not look her father in the eyes as he continued to lay plans for her future.

"I will leave your wedding trousseau for you and your aunt to decide upon. Buy what you like while we are in the city. We'll be going in tomorrow and will return here Christmas Eve morning, in time to prepare for Christmas Eve services and dinner at Don Andres' rancho.

"All that I require is that you be dressed and ready to be driven to Rancho del Dios, again a week later, on the morning of January first, to be married.

"Furthermore, I suggest that you plan a guest list and give it to Alfredo as soon as we arrive in San Diego. You may invite as many or as few guests as you desire."

With that he stepped toward the door. "It's time for the fiesta to begin." Then he turned and said sincerely, "Enjoy the day, Felicia. This party is for you. I am glad you came home. I pray that you still think so, too."

11

*T*he trail wound higher and higher up the sagebrush-covered hill behind the hacienda. Granite rocks, unearthed and pushed aside, formed a natural berm against the sharp drop to the oak-treed rancho grounds below.

Felicia had slipped away soon after the first guests started arriving, at a time she hoped she would not be missed. She needed to be alone—to think and to pray. The best place to do that was in the "secret praying place" of her childhood, around the next bend and off the trail behind two lichen-splotched boulders.

Melodic sounds of the fiesta floated upward, lifting Felicia's heavy mood. She stepped to the edge of the trail and looked down at the mass of oaks filtering the sounds rising from beneath their protective limbs. She listened carefully, smiling to herself. She could discern the high-pitched giggles of excited children, blindfolded and batting wildly at the brightly striped *pinata*, a papier-mache rooster—stuffed with candy and fresh fruit, swinging from a long hemp rope just out of reach.

She listened to the strains of stringed music drifting upward from the deeply polished violin of the strolling *mariachi*, dressed in his heavily-filigreed caballero suit and sharp silver spurs.

The background for the array of party noises was the buzz of happy voices—friends and neighbors once again enjoying a rare visit with one another.

Felicia climbed higher, around that next bend to the picture-postcard scene of the meandering creek and beyond to the vineyards, which were her father's pride. Directly below was the fish pond where she and Don Andres had tossed pebbles into the water, setting off the serious discussion of their changing world. Disappointedly, her view of the pond was blocked by a clump of sagebrush protruding from the hillside a few feet below.

Felicia moved a few steps up the winding path. Then, by wedging herself between two huge trailside boulders, she was able to lean out and peer around the clump of bushes. There it was—a bird's-eye view of the spot where Don Andres had shared his innermost fears. She leaned out a little farther, bracing her hand against the huge granite mass to her right.

Suddenly the boulder moved, throwing Felicia off-balance and tumbling her head-over-heels over the low wall. Automatically she reached out and grabbed for anything to stop her slide down the steep hillside. An instant later her fingers wrapped around the bottom limb of a wild lilac. Her grip held fast.

"Thank You, Lord," she whispered breathlessly. Still trembling from shock, Felicia managed to pull herself to her knees, then to her feet. She shook the damp sod from her plaid party skirt. Still, the mud stains of her misadventure remained.

Felcia dug her pointed-toe slippers into the soft earth and began to climb, limb over limb, to the trail twenty feet above. Then without warning her long, billowing skirt snagged on a thorny bush. She glanced over her shoulder. The entangled taffeta was beyond arm's length. Felicia bit her lip, looked ahead, and took another sure step upward. She heard the lace flounce rip from its hand-stitched border.

Only when she was climbing back over the low rock wall did Felicia notice the wad of red cloth tucked under the high side of the loose boulder. *Curious,* she thought.

Then it came to her. *It's an Indian sign of some sort. What could the secret signal mean? For what purpose is it hidden on El Camino property?*

Felicia studied the large boulder, many times

her size. Then she gave it a quick jab and was amazed how easily the tonnage jiggled in place. She bent down and examined the base more closely. Smaller rocks had been jammed under the trailside edge, tilting the giant boulder off-center. *Why?*

They were questions she could not answer, then or probably ever. One thing she did know was that she had better get back down the hill and into her room undetected to change clothes before more time lapsed. She was bound to be missed soon.

Felicia lifted her skirt to her ankles and started darting down the rain-rutted path, paying little attention to the care of her already-ruined dress. She breathed deeply, filling her lungs with fresh, December-scented air. Its winter crispness exhilarated her, as it had as a child, reminding her now, as then, of the Advent of the Christmas celebration—and with it returned the nostalgic flutter of holy anticipation.

Finally even the pins in her hair lost the battle for restraint. Once her tresses fell unleashed from the bondage of a tight bun, her long hair began to fly unhindered in the wind. She was truly home. How she loved the naturalness, the freedom of this untamed land!

Near the bottom of the hill Felicia slowed to catch her breath. *Dear Lord, You know the desire of my heart. You also know what is best for me. Deep inside I know that my father has my best interest at heart—even above those of his mysterious business deal. Lord, teach me to appreciate that which I cannot change.*

●　　●　　●

Felicia stood beside Juan Las Flores on the veranda. She smiled and offered her hand warmly as her father greeted late arrivals, Don Juan Jose Warner and his attractive wife, Dona Anita.

"Don Warner acquired the abandoned ranchos of Captain Portilla and Jose Antonio Pico, another brother of Pio Pico," her father said by way of introduction. "Trouble with the Indians scared the first owners away."

Then, turning to Warner, he asked, "The petition was for 44,323 acres, wasn't it, my friend?"

The Don, known as Juan Largo—Long John— because of his height of six feet three inches, confirmed the fact with a quick nod. "The rancho now encompasses the entire San Jose Valley, including the San Luis Rey Mission, known as Agua Caliente."

"Agua Caliente? The eleven Californios... isn't that where the hostages were taken and finally murdered?" Felicia asked innocently, brushing a loose strand away from her cheek.

The sudden silence was deafening.

"Oh, I'm very sorry...I didn't mean to..." Felicia began.

Quick-thinking Don Warner came to her rescue. "No harm done. We all mourn the deaths of the Mexican nationals, as well as the senselessness of it all. However, be assured, Senorita, our revenge will not be in kind. Don Andres and I are forming..."

Don Las Flores broke in. "Pardon me, Don Warner, ladies. I see I am being summoned to start the cockfights. Would you please excuse me?"

"Of course," smiled Don Warner. "You leave

Senorita Felicia in good hands when you leave her with us."

The three watched as Don Las Flores, aided by his cane, limped across the patio to the gaming area. "He's a fighter, your father," the Don mused. "I am proud to count him among the true patriots for law and order. There are so few Dons as corrupt-free as he and Don Andres Santiago."

Then something over the heads of the ladies caught the Don's eye. He smiled broadly and waved. "Speaking of Don Andres, here he comes now."

Felicia tensed. Before her walk she had observed her father and Don Andres engaged in a serious discussion near the bandstand. *They had to be discussing our forthcoming marriage and my attitude toward it. Surely it's the reason Don Andres has avoided me this afternoon.*

Santiago neared. Don Warner stepped back and welcomed Don Andres to their group.

Don Andres immediately acknowledged Felicia, the party's honoree, with a deep bow and a soft "Senorita."

His voice, strong and velvet-edged, sent a ripple of awareness through her. He stood so close that the silver threads of his *poncho* pricked at the sheered satin on the full sleeves of her robin-egg blue party dress. Gratefully, her hurried dress change appeared to have gone unnoticed.

Felicia raised her eyes to find Don Andres studying her. His eyes, full of expectation, searched hers for the truth of her deepest feelings.

It was Felicia who broke the spell, so with or without his answer, the Don was forced to turn his attention to Dona Warner.

"Good afternoon, Senora. You are as beautiful as ever." Then, easing into a smile, he said, "It is commonly held that you possess the secret to the fountain of youth."

Dona Warner, herself the daughter of an English sea captain Felicia had learned, had been left in the care of the Pico family while she was still a young girl. She warmed immediately to the handsome Don's flattery. She laughed lightly and remarked, "It's no secret, Don Andres. The mineral hot springs on our rancho have curative powers. The Indians discovered that secret years ago. We invite you to come and test them for yourself."

"Thank you, I accept. I am curious to learn more about the phenomenon of the sulfured hot water." Amusement flickered in his eyes. "Perhaps Senorita Las Flores would enjoy seeing the springs also. Say...after the first of the year?"

The Don's subtlety was lost on the Warners but not on Felicia. "That would be very nice," she replied graciously with controlled evenness. Still, she could not help but return his disarming smile.

"It is settled then. We will leave it to the ladies to set the exact date." Then, reaching out and putting his hand on Don Andres' shoulder, Don Warner added, "I was just about to tell Senorita Las Flores of our organizing efforts to bring law and order to our independent California."

"Good," Don Andres replied, picking up the thread of Warner's unfinished declaration. "It is our hope to seek the protection of the United States. Senorita, you probably have a better understanding than we of the Easterners' current feelings on Frontier matters. I personally feel that Don Warner's hospitality to Kearny's First Dragoons in their greatest hour of need makes him the logical spokesman to approach Washington."

"That is probably true," Felicia agreed, fanning herself with her Spanish fan to mask her quickened heartbeat. With only a trace of excitement in her voice she looked up at Don Warner and asked quizzically, "How did you help the First Dragoons?"

"I didn't," Don Warner answered sheepishly. "In fact, on the night of December second, the night the bedraggled troops arrived in the vicinity of my rancho, I was in jail myself in San Diego for consorting with the enemy. Treason they called it, I believe."

Don Andres laughed heartily and slipped his arm around Felicia, drawing her closer. He quipped with mischief-filled eyes, "Don Warner is leading you down the well-trod garden path. True, he was in jail, but he was soon exonerated. Meanwhile, his military guests back at the rancho enjoyed the first fresh meat and vegetables they had eaten in many weeks. I doubt seriously that the U.S. Army could have endured the San Pascual battle without the fortification they generously received at this 'turncoat's' rancho."

Felicia stepped from the circle of the Don's arm. "Thank heaven, they did more than endure," Felicia countered sweetly. "Tell me, Don Warner, were there many American casualties at San Pascual?"

"Eighteen officers and men were killed on the field and thirteen wounded. Among those killed were Captains Moore and Johnston of the First Dragoons. Johnston led the charge down the hill and became the first man to fall."

"I am so sorry," Felicia said, her mind's eye racing back to that night such a short time ago that she and the other stagecoach passengers were guests of the First Dragoons—and to the scene in the clearing.

"I know who Captain Johnston was. I saw him talking with Kit Carson...how did Mr. Carson fare?"

"Carson's horse, in the initial plunge into battle, stumbled and threw Carson to the ground, breaking his rifle. Carson's moment of glory came later, at Mule Hill."

Felicia felt Don Andres' eyes on her when she asked, "My aunt and I met another captain—a Fletcher Crane. Do you happen to know of his condition?"

Warner pursed his lips and scowled in thoughtful contemplation. "Crane—I recall the name. Two more Dragoons died in San Diego. Perhaps he was one of them...although I can't be sure where I heard the name used, Senorita."

Suddenly he brightened. "You'll have the answer for yourself in forty-eight hours. Our heroic officers are to be the honored guests at the Bandini dinner-dance on Tuesday evening..."

Felicia's cheeks grew suddenly hot, the voices around her turned mute, and her head began to swim. "Thank you," she murmured. "Now, if you will please excuse me, I have other guests..."

Felicia turned and ran across the grass to the hacienda, through the open double doors on the veranda, and down the hall to the privacy of her own room.

• • •

It was an hour later when a soft knock on her door awakened Felicia. She removed the cold cloth from her forehead before calling out, "Come in, please."

Aunt Winn rushed to her bedside. "Are you all right, Felicia? I should have thought to check here long before now. Your father is worried, thinking possibly that his hard stand had driven you from El Camino and delivered you into the hands of the enemy."

She placed the fingertips of one hand on Felicia's forehead and wrapped the fingers of her other around her niece's wrist.

Strangely, Mr. Jenkins' previous brow-raising comment popped into Felicia's mind. She mused to herself, *At least General Kearny identified and destroyed his adversaries. When will the Dons and their families be able to rest in that same peace?*

She started to sit up.

"Lie there a moment longer, Dear. I'm taking your pulse."

Felicia obeyed, but then confided to her aunt, "I needed to be alone for awhile. Besides, my head started to spin around and around."

Aund Winn chuckled. "I think you have your cause and effect turned around. Nevertheless, your pulse is normal. I think you'll be fine, providing you start taking seriously my advice to rest every afternoon during the hectic weeks ahead."

"I promise to do better."

"You may not realize it, but your entire body suffered the shock of your severe concussion. Recovery is a gradual process."

"I feel rested now. I think I should reappear at my own party, don't you?"

"Yes, I do, at least to thank your guests for coming. Most will be leaving soon, in order to get home before total darkness sets in. Oh, Felicia, that reminds me, Fawn Eyes has been looking for you to give you a message from Don Andres."

"What could it be? I was with him only an hour ago."

"Fawn Eyes says that you are to meet the Don at the fish pond the moment the sun sets behind Hog's Back."

"That's the purple mountain on the horizon to the west, beyond the vineyards, isn't it, Aunt Winn?"

"Yes, Dear..."

"Yes, Dear, what, Aunt Winn? Come on, I know you too well."

Aunt Winn left Felicia's bedside and walked to the window. She leaned against the tapestries and stared out across the grass-blanketed meadow. "Felicia, what answer will you give Don Andres?"

From across the room came the soft reply: "That I will marry him on the first day of January."

"Oh, Felicia..." choked Aunt Winn.

Felicia got off the bed and rushed into her aunt's arms. The two held each other close for a long time. How many times while growing up had her dear Aunt Winn comforted her? So many Felicia could not count them all.

Finally Felicia stepped back. Her eyes were

moist. "I've thought and I've prayed. It's not that I don't have a choice."

"What...what do you mean?"

"As my father would suspect of me, I could disguise myself as a boy and ride out of here. I have enough wits about me to make my way somewhere, perhaps back to Boston eventually. I considered stowing away on a whaling ship in San Diego harbor while we are in the city next week."

Felicia grinned and looked cockeyed at her beloved aunt, then said with silliness, "I even thought of dressing you in a heavy veil and marrying you off to the Don instead of me. We are the same size, you know."

Aunt Winn's eyes sparkled. "You are a survivor, Felicia. When you can find humor even in..."

"There is no humor in a loveless marriage, Aunt Winn."

The room was suddenly so still that Felicia could hear her heart pounding in her breast.

"Which brings us to the only choice worth logical consideration," stated her practical aunt firmly.

"You know me pretty well, don't you, Aunt Winn? You're right. If Captain Crane survived San Pascual and learns of my plight, perhaps he'll want to run off with..."

"Captain Crane has his own reasons for wanting you. He does not need the threat of competition to spur his ardor. Why not wait until after the dinner-dance to give your answer to Don Andres?"

Felicia sighed heavily. "Because it only makes the decision more difficult. Deep inside me, in the soul of my being, I know that it served

God's purpose in my life for me to become a qualified teacher. He has given me a burning desire to use my new skills to His glory. God directed me to this particular field of harvest. It was my destiny to come to California once we heard the news of my father's injuries. There really was no other choice. God knew that. He knows everything."

"I do not mean to play the devil's advocate, but many Captains' wives are contributing members to society, wherever their husbands are billeted, Felicia."

"I know, Aunt Winn, but there's more to it."

"What? Tell me."

"Everything bad I heard about Don Andres has been dispelled. The remaining mysteries are secrets from *me*, but not from my father. I truly believe my father when he says that, aside from their private business deal, Don Andres would be his first choice for my husband."

"Felicia, what is the color of Don Andres' eyes?"

Felicia giggled. "Chocolate brown—you know that."

"And his spiritual tone?"

"He's a Christian, Aunt Winn. He wants to use his power for peace on the Frontier. There he has my respect."

"What do you mean by 'there'? Where doesn't he?"

"He holds with the barbaric 'right' to purchase a wife. I cannot respect his attitude, no matter how deeply ingrained it is in his heritage."

Felicia clung to her aunt one more time be-

fore concluding, "Don Andres will be my husband. I will respect him—but I will never love
him."

12

*S*he saw Don Andres waiting by the pond before he heard her footsteps on the path and looked up. Felicia walked closer before he came—with hesitation, she thought, to meet her. There was a look of apprehension in his eyes.

Without a word the Don took her arm and slipped it possessively through his. Felicia allowed her body to lean into his as they walked past the row of poinsettias to the exact spot

by the pond where they had talked earlier.
The solidness of his step gave her a sense of
comfort.

Felicia waited silently for Don Andres to speak.
*What could have possibly happened within the
last hour to necessitate this secret meeting?* she
wondered. Something was definitely troubling
him.

Finally she broke the awkward silence by com-
menting, "See how the fish seem to lose the
vividness of color when the sun leaves their
backs?"

Don Andres looked at her quizzically. "I do not
wish to sound impolite, Felicia, but what is the
'desperate concern' which was the subject of your
urgent note?"

"Note? What note?" She looked at him discon-
certedly.

"The note handed to me soon after you disappeared through the veranda doors. It read that
I was to wait for you here at the pond—that it was
a matter of life and death."

"Don Andres, I penned no note," she corrected with firmness. "I am here because Fawn
Eyes sent a message through my Aunt Winn that
you wished to meet me here the moment the sun
set..."

The Don's face clouded with uneasiness. His
dark eyes narrowed, and with the hardness of
flint he scanned the parklike setting around
them.

"We appear to be alone," Don Andres whispered.

"I'm sure we are, as was surely the intent of
Cupid's helper who arranged this clandestine
meeting."

Felicia lowered her dark lashes as color filled

her cheeks. "I suspect my aunt's hand in this over-dramatic shenanigan."

"Are you certain?" he asked seriously.

"Who or what else could it be?" she responded lightly.

"The note could have a more sinister origin."

"Like...?"

"A trap." His eyes darted nervously, surveying the thick foliage on the other side of the pond.

"If so, wouldn't it have sprung by now?"

"Hopefully, you're right. It's probably, as you suggest, a harmless prank."

Only then did she feel the Don release his guard and return his attention to her.

"Few know, least of all your aunt, of the cloak-and-dagger games—the spy missions in disguise—used lately by all sides to gain the advantage over the enemy."

"But the war is over in San Diego!" she protested. Too late Felicia then thought of the eleven men...

"Is it, Felicia?" His eyes darkened with emotion. Something intense flared between them.

Her quickening heart understood the battle-ground of his concern, and Felicia was suddenly aware of the heat of his body next to hers.

"Stay with me a few moments," he pleaded huskily. "You have your rosy cheeks back. You must be feeling better."

"Yes, I am, thank you." His nearness was overwhelming. A hot tingling feeling raced through her veins. She tried to pretend not to notice.

"I rested for awhile. Aunt Winn convinced

me that I must consider my recovery program much more seriously. She made me promise to rest every afternoon from now until the—"

"The evening of the Bandinis' Christmas dinner-dance, I suppose. I hope after you see Captain Crane in the living flesh you will begin to relax and apply your energy to more meaningful matters."

Felicia stepped back. "How dare you!" Her dark eyes flashed angrily.

"Another burr under the saddle? How many more are there, Felicia?"

The smoldering look in his eyes only incensed her more.

"Life for me on this planet did not begin the moment of ambush, nor did it for you, I'm sure. I have acquired a host of friends whom I care enough to inquire about."

She could not keep the tremble from her voice. "Captain Crane is one of those responsible for saving us from an Indian attack. Certainly I cannot be faulted for seeking knowledge of his temporal well-being."

The Don stiffened as though she had struck him. "Your point is well-taken. Forgive me. I am wearing my jealousy on my sleeve, as you Americans say it."

She took a quick breath of utter astonishment. "You—jealous? Of my..." Her almost inaudible voice broke off in midsentence. She was surprised once again by this unpredictable man.

They were standing separately now, along the fence railing. Don Andres stared out over the water when he asked, "Have you given thought to my question, Felicia?"

"Yes," she replied distantly. Felicia was still dazed, trying to assimilate the Don's open admittance of jealousy. A war of intense emotions raged within her. She had to know...

"Why is our marriage part of a business deal with my father? Were you me, wouldn't you want to know?" She also addressed some far-off lily pad instead of him directly.

"Yes, I would," he replied. Then he said no more. An unwelcome tension built between them.

The interminable silence dragged on. Felicia tried to swallow the lump rising in her throat. But the confusion that had controlled her life these past weeks at last overwhelmed her. She found herself trying to bite back tears that refused to be contained a moment longer.

Deep sobs wracked her insides. She gulped hard. Hot tears slipped down her cheeks. Finally she wept aloud, uncontrollably.

Suddenly Don Andres' arms wrapped around her, engulfing her. Even in her misery she welcomed the aroma of his body, the warmth of his closeness. She buried her face against his chest and continued to sob.

He held her close a long time, rubbing her shoulders and back as one would to comfort a forlorn child.

"Felicia, does it matter that I have paid dearly for the privilege of your hand in marriage? Your dowry is not in dollars. It is in value received for honor, dignity, protection. Your father and I have pledged a merger of our ranchos, strengthening our position for justice on the Frontier. Only our marriage can make our mutual pledge a reality."

He sighed heavily. "Some things in life, Felicia, are too valuable to appraise in gold."

She looked up at him. Tears still clung to the tips of her long lashes, shining like the first stars in the twilight.

"I will obey my father and honor his pledge and marry you," Felicia said simply, without emotion.

There were no more words. His lips pressed against hers, devouring their quivering softness.

Felicia's head began to spin wildly. She was shocked at her own eager response to the touch of the Don's lips. She vainly tried to pull back.

She felt the heady sensation of his lips against her ear... her neck...

Then from over the Don's shoulder came a heavy crashing sound and the low-pitched snapping of thick limbs. Startled, Felicia looked up.

"Look out!" she screamed.

In the next instant Felicia's mind captured in slow motion the fearful image of the huge boulder, weighing tons, picking up momentum as it ripped down the steep hillside, pulverizing all vegetation that it did not send flying in every direction with the speed of a catapult.

It was headed straight for them!

The instant Felicia screamed she pushed Don Andres out of harm's way—with strength she did not normally possess. Had he taken time to turn around he would have been struck dead.

The monstrous boulder tore past them and through the fence. It splashed harmlessly into the fish pond, sending a tidal wave of water surging toward the opposite shore.

Felicia instinctively knew where to look. Her

eyes were quick enough to catch a fleeting glimpse of a brave's feather disappearing on the trail high above.

Then, once again, she was in the Don's arms.

"Thank you, my darling. Is it any wonder I fell madly in love with you the moment you stepped to the door of the stagecoach? You had the same fire in your eyes then as you do now."

13

"*T*his certainly isn't Boston," whispered Aunt Winn as their carriage groped its way along the dark, mud-rutted street.

"Where is your charity, Aunt Winn?" Felicia teased. "Remember, there are fewer than fifty houses in the whole pueblo. Given time, San Diego will rival your Eastern port in industry and in cultural richness. Mark my words."

Aunt Winn laughed. "If it happens, much of the

credit will fall to the Bandinis. Imagine them, opening up their home almost every night of the week for a gala ball!"

"Imagine having ten children, each with his or her own Indian maid!" Felicia giggled. She nudged her aunt playfully as their coach rounded a corner. "How about the Arguellos family with twenty-two?"

"Look, Felicia, here we are," interrupted Aunt Winnifred, excited by the appearance of the carriage-lined street. A minute later their driver pulled to a stop at the front entrance of the low, rambling, thick-walled and festively lighted Bandini house.

Don Las Flores stepped out to speak to the driver. Felicia reached across the coach and straightened a ruffle caught under Aunt Winn's lace shawl. "You do look fetching, Auntie," she said, squeezing her aunt's hand.

Winnifred Worthington held on to Felicia's hand. "This is a big evening for you, Dear. Do not let anything dull the diamond sparkle in your eyes or dampen the joyous expectation in your heart."

"Aunt Winn," she whispered, "I know that he may not be here, even if he survived the battle without a scratch."

"If Captain Crane is here, my sweet, remember that his uniform will be more tattered and worn than when you said good-bye. He's been sleeping in a drafty Mexican garrison, and although he has had an abundance of beef and mutton, his diet has been void of fresh fruits and vegetables. He's likely to appear more gaunt..."

"Aunt Winn, please don't worry. Perhaps the dream is already over. He may not remember me with any special fondness. After all, he's been in the city for more than a week. He's probably found..."

"That's nonsense!" her aunt exclaimed. "You and I both know it. What I'm saying, Felicia, is enjoy being Cinderella this one evening."

"I do feel like Cinderella arriving at a grand ball." Then she sighed pensively, "And, like Cinderella, I will leave at the stroke of midnight without Prince Charming—the love chapter in my life closed forever. For in a matter of days I will marry Don Andres."

"Unless your father changes his mind after meeting Captain Crane..."

"No, Aunt Winn. Nothing will change now. I too have given my word of honor to Don Santiago."

Aunt Winn sighed, "Life is not over, Felicia. God does not intend for us to see all things clearly. Trust Him."

Then, slipping into a lighter mood, Aunt Winn touched a lace-gloved fingertip under Felicia's dainty chin and gently raised it the tiniest bit. "There, that's more becoming a lady."

Felicia smiled. "Thanks, Aunt Winn. How do I look? I want my father to be proud of me."

"You're absolutely beautiful! I'm glad that you decided to wear the black lace over yellow taffeta. It's daring. Every other woman will be dressed in some combination of red and green."

"The flowers? Should I remove them from my hair? Perhaps the yellow hibiscuses are too much."

"Leave them. They're perfect against your

black hair. I especially like them nestled low on your neck in the bun below your ear. It's not only very fashionable, but looks youthful."

One minute and a whispered prayer later, Felicia and her aunt stepped from the carriage to the sound of waltz music floating through the balmy night air.

"You're right, Aunt Winn," Felicia teased under her breath, "even the December weather isn't Boston's."

"Are you ready, ladies?" Don Juan asked, stepping between the two. He was handsomely dressed in a dark blue English-cut long coat and trousers. He wore his jacket open, revealing the white corded-cotton vest that Aunt Winn brought him from Boston. His dark-blue cravat was fastened with an exquisite jeweled brooch, his wedding gift from Felicia's mother.

The familiar aroma of his lingering pipe tobacco renewed the gratefulness in Felicia's heart and brought a smile to her lips. She was ready to take her father's arm and meet San Diego's society.

The great hall was festooned exactly as she had pictured, with a profusion of fresh evergreens and wild red berries. Massive bouquets of Christmas-red poinsettias in handwoven Mexican baskets decorated out-of-the-way corners. A huge, ornate Mexican silver candelabra, holding a host of brightly lighted candles, formed a centerpiece for the lavish spread on the main table.

The room was crowded with ladies in bell-skirted, shining satins and taffetas and with men attired much like her father in elegantly styled English suits. Among the guests were an equal number of military officers, most in pale-blue trousers and dark-blue jackets with yellow braid. Even from across the room Felicia could see that the uniforms were in worse condition than Aunt Winn had predicted. However, Felicia also noticed that the men in blue stood as straight and proud as the yellow stripe down their trouser seams.

There were a few men in uniforms different from those of the officers of the Army of the West. *They must be officers from the ships in the harbor—the Cyane, Congress, Savannah, and Portsmouth.*

Surely the presence of 600 additional sailors and Marines in the area hastened Mexico's capitulation of San Diego—allowing Kearny and his men a safe haven following the battle of San Pascual. Peace in San Diego by Christmas. Praise God! He always does provide according to His will.

"Help me to remember that in my impatience, Lord," Felicia mused almost inaudibly.

She looked carefully at the guests milling around the punch table and at those visiting in small groups. She caught a quick glimpse of the two couples strolling arm-in-arm toward the room where the United States Sixth Regimental Infantry Band played yet another waltz for their entertainment.

He's not here. Don Warner recollected correctly: Captain Crane is dead!

Felicia vaguely remembered Don Juan introducing her to their host and hostess before excusing himself to get her and Aunt Winn a glass of punch. She declined. Her stomach was fluttering enough without adding to it the syrupy sweetness of holiday punch.

Suddenly there was a touch at her elbow. Tingles ran up Felicia's spine. She hesitated, then turned and slowly raised her eyes. Her breath caught in her throat.

"Miss Worthington—Felicia?"

"Julius Jenkins! How wonderful to see you," Felicia's voice was thin, but her words were sincerely offered. She extended her hand. At the same moment, Ophelia Jenkins and Aunt Winn greeted each other with broad smiles and a warm embrace. Then they all began talking at once.

"I've thought of you two often," Felicia said, "and prayed that the remaining leg of your journey into San Diego was without incident."

Ophelia looked to her husband.

"Well, almost. . . ." he answered, then stopped abruptly.

"Go ahead, Julius. It won't hurt to talk about it now, seeing that the lady's safe and all."

The smile left Felicia's face. "What happened, Julius?"

Jenkins motioned the ladies to lean closer. He looked around quickly, and, finding no one within earshot, bent forward and whispered loudly, "Would you believe it? Another ambush—just like the first."

"What do you mean, just like the first?" asked Aunt Winnifred.

"This time it was a posse of masked men who wanted her—the 'senorita worth gold,' they called Miss Worthington."

"We had no idea you were such an important person, Miss Worthington," Ophelia Jenkins whispered apologetically. "Julius shouldn't have said what he did about his refusing to travel with a Mexican woman..."

Felicia reached over and patted Ophelia's hand. "No matter. I should have told you at the outset who I was. However, at the time I really didn't think it would matter in the way that it did."

"What happened when you couldn't produce Felicia?" Aunt Winn was not about to let the matter rest.

Jenkins looked stunned—as if the question were not a logical one to ask.

"Please tell us," Felicia pressed in a hard whisper. "I can tell that it must be something awful or you wouldn't..."

After a pause, Julius conceded.

"Shotgun Sam got a bit impatient with the men, thinking he could smart-mouth them because you were no longer aboard. One of the bandits, frustrated, I guess, by Sam gloating that they had got to the henhouse too late, up and shot poor Sam, hitting him right in the chest..."

"Oh, no!" Felicia pressed her hand against her breast to still her throbbing heart. "Is he...is he...?"

"Dead? No, thank our Lord for nothing less than a miracle. Soon as Sam was hit, the gang took off over the nearest hill. We're sure they think that Sam was mortally wounded.

"That's partly why we agreed with the driver not to say a word—for Sam's protection as well as for your safety and ours. Sam's recovering at his brother's place a little south of here.

"We hope that the bandits think a murder

charge awaits them if they return to these parts,'' concluded Jenkins.

''And we had no idea what happened to you,'' interjected his wife. ''You could have been killed, for all we knew. It's an answer to our prayers to see you here.'' Ophelia Jenkins looked for a moment as if she might cry. She reached for her husband's offered handkerchief.

''Truthfully—the ambush was the most frightening event of my life. Later I learned that the scene had been orchestrated by my father, who evidently had advance warning of the second ambush attempt you describe.''

''Believe us, Felicia,'' Jenkins whispered most seriously, ''the second group of thugs were the most unsavory I've ever seen. If they had gotten hold of you...''

''Let's get off this depressing subject,'' Ophelia insisted with a quick shiver. ''You spoke of your father, Felicia. How is he?''

''Wonderful—all but recovered from his injuries, thank you. He should be joining us in a moment or two. It will give me pleasure to introduce him to you.''

Felicia glanced toward the punch table, wondering what could be keeping her father.

''I hope that it is me for whom you are looking,'' a familiar voice whispered close to her ear. She could feel his warm breath on her neck.

Felicia spun around.

He stood there devastatingly handsome, gazing down at her with eyes as green, as soft as sea foam—a perfect vision of a tender memory.

Felicia smiled up at him wide-eyed, almost disbelieving. In her hope she had planned

what she would say, should they meet—yet in
this magical moment the words would not
come.

He looked down at her with a smile as intimate
as a kiss.

Felicia reached up and with a quivering fingertip gently traced the scar that ran the length
of his cheek to his square-cut jawline. Her
dark eyes danced and her black hair shimmered
in the ricocheting candlelight.

"You are alive and well," she murmured in
sweet confirmation, sliding her hand down the
front of his jacket against the yellow braid to the
place where his heart beat fiercely behind the
brass buttons.

Then, suddenly embarrassed by her action,
Felicia withdrew her hand and stepped back. She
turned. The others were gone, melted into the
crowd.

"Felicia, I have thought of you night and
day..."

"And what were those thoughts, Captain?" she
responded shyly.

"Of anticipation, of frustration. Felicia, I asked
everywhere. No one knew of a Worthington family living in the area at this time. I was all but convinced that you were a figment of my tortured
imagination."

Then Crane reached into his jacket and withdrew from near his heart the lace handkerchief
that Felicia had given him during their last
moments together. He held it lovingly in the palm
of his hand.

"This token, this tangible keepsake, helped me
retain my sanity..."

"Good evening, Senorita...Captain."

It was Don Warner.

"I hope I am not intruding, but dinner has been announced." Don Warner looked to Felicia and said, "Your father is embroiled in a discussion over the price of hides. He asked me to find you and tell you that he is escorting your aunt into dinner. If you would care to join..."

"I will be escorting the lady, Sir," Captain Crane said pleasantly but firmly.

The Don looked to Felicia for confirmation. "Thank my father for his concern, but Captain Crane..."

The Don's eyes brightened with interest. "So you are the mysterious and heroic Captain Crane. I'm delighted to meet you, Sir."

Don Warner extended his hand, but was stopped for an awkward moment until Crane transferred Felicia's lace handkerchief to his other hand.

Crane said to Warner as they shook hands, "Heroism, like beauty, is often in the eye of the beholder. If I was ever a hero, Sir, it was to honor this mysterious beauty, whose token of esteem I carried into battle."

Felicia felt her knees weaken with the sudden racing of her heart. "Captain, you flatter me beyond understanding..."

Then, with downcast eyes, Felicia could feel the anguished brown eyes piercing through the shallowness of her words, seeking reason for her betrayal.

Minutes later, when Fletcher Crane seated Felicia at dinner, he scanned the room and asked, "Where is your father seated? I feel at a disadvantage..."

Her composure regained, Felicia laughed lightly. "Father knows I am well able to care for myself. However, I look forward to your meeting one another. Perhaps, later during the dancing...oh, I see him. Look through the doorway into the other room. He's the bearded one, standing. I believe he is toasting my aunt.''

Captain Crane smiled approvingly. "He looks like a respectable American citizen—unusual for these parts.''

What an odd remark, thought Felicia.

Dinner was served without evidence of short rations in any course. An imaginative menu of green corn tamales, *arroz-con-pollo* (a form of barbequed chicken in a cream sauce), rice from China, and sliced beef filled the most hearty eater.

Felicia had little inclination and even less time to touch the food on her plate. Fletcher Crane asked one question after another concerning every moment of her life since they parted three weeks earlier on that cold morning in the wind-whipped saddle of the mountain.

Felicia was telling him of the Don's ambush when Crane startled her by interrupting.

"Abducted by a Mexican! It's fortunate that you weren't violated and murdered!" Crane's words, fired in anger, were heard only by Felicia.

Still, Felicia's face flushed with sudden color. "It ended well. I am here tonight,'' she reminded him sweetly. "The ambush turned out to be a ploy by my father to prevent a second, more tragic...''

"Your father would engage and trust his daughter's safety to a Mexican national? Unfathomable!''

Felicia swallowed hard and picked up her fork. She took a few bites, then asked, "Now that you've seen the span of lower California—the deserts, mountains, and blue Pacific—what do you think of the land of your conquest?"

"Truthfully?"

Felicia nodded, not realizing herself how the soft candlelight accented the loveliness of her alabaster skin.

"In truth, I agree with Senator Daniel Webster of Massachusetts—'Not worth a dollar.' "

"Fletcher Crane, are you serious?" Felicia thought surely the handsome Captain must be joking.

"Dear Felicia, Webster doesn't like the scenery. For me, it's the people—present company excluded, of course."

"People?"

"One expects to encounter savages in unexplored territory. But here, they live half-tamed among the city residents. And for the most part, I find that the city fathers themselves are a collection of Latin-Indian half-breeds, some only a generation removed from the savage state."

Felicia looked at her dinner partner incredulously. A shadow was moving across her harvest-moon vision.

"Excluding the Indians, every person living in the United States has his roots in a foreign country..." she replied defensively, a dull ache beginning to invade the secret place in her heart.

"A *civilized* foreign country, Felicia. I say, leave this land to the natives. What good to the U.S. is this vast territory teaming with primitive life? California will become a burden upon the taxpayers of our country."

"I look at California as a challenge—its land and its people. We have the opportunity to carve out, to share, to—"

"You've been here too long, darling—you're beginning to sound like one of them," he broke in with disgust.

What was happening? She had dreamed of this man, but the two of them did not share the same dream.

Just then dessert was set in front of them—a local favorite: Spanish flan with liquored caramel sauce.

"What is flan?" whispered Crane in Felicia's ear. She pretended not to notice his flimsy excuse to move closer to her.

She smiled warily and replied, "It's a form of custard. Extremely popular in Spain and Mexico. You may not learn to like the people, but you'll grow to love our cooking once you've been here awhile."

He put down his spoon. "Let's leave our desserts and dance while the floor is not crowded, shall we?" His eyes beckoned hers magnetically.

Once in his arms and whirling around the highly polished plank floor of the ballroom, Crane confided, "Felicia, I won't be here long enough to learn to like Mexican cooking. We're marching north in a few days, before the year's end."

Felicia stopped dancing and looked up into his longing eyes.

Without another word passing between them, he led her from the dance floor and out onto the veranda.

The night sky was electrified with stars. Still,

Crane's eagerness no longer excited her—it unsettled her.

"Felicia," he began, lightly fingering a loose tendril of hair on her cheek, "I cannot bear the thought of you staying in this God-forsaken place a day longer than you must. Marry me, then return with your aunt to Boston and wait for me there."

Felicia's heart fluttered wildly in her breast. This was the moment she had dreamed of—from that instant in the stagecoach when his eyes, the color of green ice, caught and held hers captive—until now, another magical moment shared under California stars.

She knew when she stepped from the carriage earlier this evening that she could never marry this man of her dreams. Her destiny was promised. She intended to tell Fletcher the reason, should they reach this deja vu moment.

Suddenly it was clear to Felicia that her father's contract with Don Andres was not the reason she was declining Fletcher Crane's proposal—and she would not use it as an excuse!

Felicia stepped back purposefully. Crane took her hands into his.

"Fletcher, Boston is not my home. My roots are here. I was destined to stay here before we met. California is my home."

Crane moved quickly to gather her into his arms.

Felicia pushed him away gently but firmly. "Hear me out, Fletcher, before I lose the courage to say all that I must."

Crane released her and took her hands into his own once again.

Felicia continued. "There is work to be done here. I have the skill to teach children's minds—

minds that hunger for basic knowledge, minds that must be taught the elementary skills that 'civilized Bostonians' take for granted.''

''Felicia,'' Crane scoffed, ''you are a dreamer. If not, you are too much of a lady to lower yourself to deal with the scrawny, wild-eyed offspring of—''

''Half-breeds?'' Felicia finished for him.

''Yes! You could never hope to understand their backward culture, their—''

''Their prejudices? Their frustration with white men's lies? Or perhaps their anger over land stolen from them by fair-minded, civilized Christian—''

''Felicia Worthington! What are you saying? You're taking the side of the pagan savages! I forbid it!'' Crane's face was white with anger.

In a voice completely calm, Felicia responded simply, ''The answer is no, Fletcher. I will not marry you. I am proud of my heritage—I am a half-breed, a *Christian* savage, if you will.''

Crane reached out and pulled her roughly to him. His fingers dug into her arms. He spoke warningly through clenched teeth. The green in his eyes hardened to ice. ''Don't jest with me, my love. I will not tolerate such insolence.''

Felicia pushed away, her heart pounding with the colliding emotions of pride and disappointment.

''You saw my father—Yankee-born. My mother was the Spanish niece of a Mexican governor. You searched for me in vain because, until yesterday, I was staying with my father at Rancho El Camino. Here in California I am known as

Felicia Maria Las Flores, daughter of Don Juan Las Flores.''

Captain Fletcher Crane dropped his arms listlessly to his sides. His shoulders slumped. ''I never would have guessed—you are so beautiful, so well-educated.''

It was as if he were speaking to himself—as truly he was. For Felicia had turned and walked back into the ballroom—her chin held high, just as Aunt Winn had shown her.

14

"**D**o you think I should put this plaid taffeta skirt in the Christmas charity box, Aunt Winn? The housekeeper has mended it beautifully."

"Of course, Dear. Everything in your trousseau must be new. Keep nothing that Don Andres has seen before."

"Open both of my trunks, please, Fawn Eyes. We've got to hurry if we are to have the Christmas charity box filled and be ready, too, by three o'clock this afternoon to start out for Rancho del Dios."

Aunt Winn mused aloud, "When I get back to Boston, I'm going to tell my pastor of Don Andres' wonderful tradition of bringing unneeded clothing and surplus food to Christmas Eve services."

Fawn Eyes offered in her small voice, " 'Each person can find something to share with another, no matter how little each one has,' says the Don."

"He is so right, Fawn Eyes," smiled Felicia. "This year I have more than enough to share. So let's start filling the box."

"What happens to the packages placed under the Christmas tree during the service, Fawn Eyes?" asked Aunt Winn, who was matching pairs of lace gloves in her lap.

"The freshly baked goods and the fruits and vegetables are taken before midnight to poor Indians that the Don's rancheros have told him about. The Don gives meat from his cattle; sometimes the gift to one large family will fill a carreta. The caballeros who deliver the gifts then have a party for themselves that lasts the rest of the night. For that reason the Don chooses only unmarried caballeros to take the gifts. He doesn't want fathers to be away from their families on Christmas Eve."

"Is Don Andres well-liked by his people?" Felicia asked sweetly.

"He is the best Don there is!" replied the young girl proudly.

Felicia caught Aunt Winn's "get-to-work" look. She winked back and then set to the task at hand.

First Felicia pulled from the trunk her dark-brown traveling suit. "This old thing has a cross-country store of memories woven into it . . ."

"Out it goes, Felicia. Remember, I bought you several new things in San Diego the day after the Bandinis' party. You have more than ample, considering that the clothes in those trunks were new when you left Boston and most haven't yet been unpacked since our arrival in California."

"What's its memory, Senorita?" Fawn Eyes asked, caressing the smooth black velvet trim on the cuff of Felicia's worn-thin traveling dress.

"I was wearing it when Don Andres ambushed us," she replied distantly.

Felicia shook out the green-and-red muslin with the white collar. She remembered she was wearing it when the masked bandito—Don Andres—kissed her while they were alone in the chapel. Felicia folded the dress and put it into the box without saying a word to the others.

Felicia's fingers began to tremble as she reached into the trunk for the next garment—the mint-green walking dress. She pressed it quickly to her breast. She could not muffle his fiery words: "Who chose Adam's wife?" Felicia handed the gown silently to Fawn Eyes.

"What about this ball gown, Senorita?"

Felicia looked up from where she was kneeling in front of the trunk.

"Oh, that, Fawn Eyes. Don Andres has never seen me in that yellow-taffeta-and-black-lace and he never will! Discard it. It is the same ball gown I wore to the Bandinis' Christmas party."

Aunt Winn's silence at the moment was appreciated. Felicia had told her aunt, over a cup of hot milk before bed, every word of what had transpired earlier that evening between her and Captain Crane. Aunt Winn's first comment had been, "Memories are precious. Cherish the best, learn from the rest."

Felicia returned to the trunk, pulling out her robin-egg satin—the party dress she had worn the last hour of the fiesta given in her honor. Felicia examined the dress closely. She turned it toward the light. A tear stain on the bodice?

Swirling to the forefront of her mind was the scene that took place in this very room, when she had cried out to her aunt, "He is a Christian. He wants to use his power for peace . . . he will have my respect but not my love."

Felicia buried her head in the satin softness of the perfume-scented gown and let the fresh tears flow. Only then did she admit to herself that had Captain Crane been the man of her dreams he would have been wearing a serape. She knew in her heart, too, that Don Warner's eyes were gray. The anguished brown eyes that searched her heart for truth, on more than one occasion, belonged to the man who had said, "I fell madly in love with you the moment you stepped to the door of the stagecoach."

Felicia threw aside the dress, ran to Aunt Winn, and buried her head in her favorite aunt's lap.

"I've been such an arrogant fool, haven't I?" she sobbed. "I deserve Captain Crane for a husband. That should be my punishment."

"Felicia, Felicia!" Aunt Winn was both laughing

and crying at the same time. "You've been no greater fool than I. Thinking back, I advised you poorly at every turn. Fortunately, God does not heed my counsel, for love has its own destiny."

"Aunt Winn, I *do* love Don Andres. I love him with all my heart!"

15

*T*he sun was setting against a salmon, mackerel-backed sky when they crested the last hill and Don Las Flores pulled the carriage to a halt.

"There it is, Felicia, the breathtakingly beautiful Rancho del Dios—a land grant with rich grazing lands, natural lakes, pure springs, and a fine vineyard beyond that grove of black oaks to the north. It's home to thousands of head of cattle, hundreds of Indians, and one Don Andres Santiago.''

Felicia leaned her head against her father's shoulder. There was detectable wistfulness in her voice. ''In a week's time, Rancho del Dios will become my home also. The next time we make this trip, Father, it will be on my wedding day.''

''How do you feel about that, Felicia?'' her father asked, his eyes fixed on a spot somewhere in the valley. ''Do you still despise me for forcing you into an unwanted marriage?''

Felicia sat up in alarm. Her father turned to face her. His beard seemed whiter, his blue eyes dull.

Felicia slipped her arms around her father's neck and laid her head against his chest. ''I have never despised you—not for an instant in my entire life. Since the day I was born I've loved and respected you with my whole heart.''

''However...'' Don Juan began contrarily.

''However,'' Felicia admitted, ''I was angry and desperately frightened over the prospect of spending the rest of my life chained to a barbarian about whom I knew very little—and what I thought I knew wasn't good.

''All I've ever wanted is to someday have a Christian husband I could love and respect—as much as my mother loved and respected you. I wanted to promise my heart to a man who would love and cherish me, as you did your wife.''

''I know, Felicia. That's the prayer your mother and I had for all of our daughters.''

''I didn't see how it could all come together in a business contract between land baron Don Las Flores and a stranger of questionable reputation.''

The Don's voice was hesitant. "You use the past tense...you say you *were* angry. Have you forgiven me?"

"Father, it is I who begs your forgiveness. Deep in my heart I knew all along that you would never 'sell me to the highest bidder.'

"In defense, all I can say is that it was a perilous journey across the country. I prayed constantly during those long weeks that we would arrive safely and find you defying the odds by recovering from the wounds of the Indian attack.

"Then, within hours of reaching your bedside, I was abducted by a masked bandito—who declared that he had purchased me as his wife!

"Aunt Winn and I secretly escaped from Rancho del Dios because we thought we were being held captive. We still had no idea if you were dead or alive."

"That too was my doing." Don Juan tucked his daughter closer. A lone tear ran down his face and splashed onto Felicia's cheek, mixing with her own tears.

"Felicia, my precious, I never looked at our plan to confound the enemy from your point of view. My heart aches with the anguish I have caused both you and my dear sister."

"I know that all you did was for our protection—you and Don Andres risked your lives to assure ours. I...I love you both so very much."

The Don drew back and looked deeply into Felicia's dark eyes. "You say that you *love* Don Andres?"

The tears running down Felicia's face and those clinging to her long lashes danced like cut crystal in the twilight. "Oh, yes, Father. I've grown to love him—as much as mother loved you on your wedding day."

"Does...does he know that, Felicia?" her father probed gently.

"No, but he will. I intend to tell him so tonight."

Don Las Flores reached up and unfastened the jeweled brooch from his cravat. He put it in Felicia's hand and closed her fingers over it.

"Tell him with this—the perfect Christmas gift for a bride to give her groom."

"Oh, Father, I cannot accept this brooch, nor will Don Andres. It was a present from my mother to you."

"We called it our 'love gift,' " he said. "It was always your mother's wish that I would pass the brooch on to the first of our daughters who found such a love as ours."

Then he smiled through dampened eyes and quipped, "I was beginning to think I might be keeping it long enough to be buried wearing it."

Felicia hugged her father. "Thank you for loving me and for your patience with me. A blessed Christmas to you, Father."

Then from out of the silence came the sound of squeaking wheels.

"Your aunt's carriage with Fawn Eyes and the others is gaining on us. The carretas with gifts can't be far behind. It's time we moved on. I'll have you at the chapel within ten minutes. Can you wait that long to see your love?"

"Ten minutes and no more," she laughed gaily.

However, Felicia's schedule did not go as planned. Upon their arrival, no sooner had Don Juan helped Felicia from the carriage when a young Indian boy ran up with the message that Don Santiago wanted to see Don Las Flores, privately, as soon as possible.

"Wait here for your aunt," her father advised. "She will be along within a minute or two. I'll go now and see what Don Andres has on his mind. Save us places in the front row of the chapel."

Felicia did as she was told.

The chapel was filled and the services beginning before Don Andres and her father settled into the pew beside her. Felicia smiled at the recollection that this was the same pew in which Don Andres had startled her in his bandito disguise.

The Don's coal-black suit was the perfect complement for Felicia's red satin gown with its tiers of black lace on the skirt and on the wide, shoulder-edge neckline. She wore a high, jeweled Spanish comb at the crown of her head. Over it cascaded a black lace mantilla, demurely covering the bareness of her neck and shoulders.

Felicia looked up at the chiseled profile of the proud Don sitting next to her and thought, *All that highly polished sterling silver adorning your festival suit does not outshine the love I have for you, Don Andres.*

It was a Christmas Eve service that Felicia could hardly endure—her happiness was so complete. The padre, dressed in his simple surplus tied with a cord around the waist of his lanky frame, delivered a message that spoke directly to Felicia's heart.

"For unto whomsoever much is given, of him shall be much required; and to whom men have committed much, of him they will ask more."

Felicia saw clearly God's hand in her life. Her love for this land, her education—even her mixed parentage—was a gift of God to prepare her perfectly for the role of Don Andres' wife and helpmate.

Separately, we each have a dream for this land, these people. Together, we can make that dream a reality...

Felicia's attention was brought back to the moment by the movement of people leaving their seats. She watched as the rancheros, caballeros, and even Dons and their families filed up to the front of the chapel and placed "gifts of sharing" under the tall, fresh evergreen, decorated with pine cones, candles, and strings of berries and popcorn.

She saw Fawn Eyes walk past. Her gaze followed the blossoming young girl. *How beautifully her long hair shines!* Felicia thought. Then she saw Fawn Eyes dip into her pocket and pull out her gift. It was the inlaid hairbrush Felicia had given her!

Felicia gasped as the young girl placed her mother's heirloom lovingly among the other gifts beneath the tree.

Don Andres leaned over and whispered into Felicia's veil. "It is her one possession. It's the first time she has something of her own to share."

Felicia could barely see through her glistening eyes.

"Once again, she has given wholly of herself for another. I have so much to learn from these people," Felicia whispered.

"And you have so much to share with them. That is what life is all about, my love."

The mere touch of his hand against hers sent a warming shiver through her body.

They stood to sing the closing hymn: "Hark! the herald angels sing, Glory to the newborn King! Peace on earth and mercy mild. . ."

Then, while the congregation hummed the final verse, the worshipers left the church row by row, beginning with the front pew.

Don Andres led Felicia down the center aisle and out of the chapel. They walked to the edge of darkness. There they stopped, and Don Andres carefully lifted Felicia's veil from her face.

His gaze was as soft as a caress. It bore into her in silent expectation.

Felicia's heart danced with excitement.

Don Andres leaned down and kissed her on the tip of her nose. "A blessed Christmas to you, my love."

He took her arm in his and they started up to the path to the brightly lighted hacienda, where the Don's staff had prepared a lavish Christmas dinner for his guests.

When they met the fork in the path, the Don suggested, "We have a few minutes before the guests gather. Let's walk up to the lookout together. There is something I want to tell you."

Without waiting for her reply, he guided Felicia to the stony point overlooking the chapel below.

He reached out to her in the darkness and Felicia walked willingly into his arms, realizing then how her body longed for his touch.

"My love, I spoke to your father earlier... I have decided to cancel our wedding."

"Until when?" Even in the darkness Felicia lowered her lashes to hide her hurt.

"Forever."

The words struck hard. A flash of disappointment ripped through her. She felt her body go limp in his arms.

"After Christmas I will meet and renegotiate with my greed-filled cousins, who will not stop short of death to acquire your father's rancho, which separates their holdings at the eastern boundary. There's also an age-old Indian rumor of gold near that eastern boundary."

"Gold! Then it was your cousins who staged the Indian raid on Rancho El Camino—the raid that nearly cost my father his life?"

"Yes, my love. Once Don Las Flores and I made a contract to join our ranchos through marriage, my cousins' advances on your father's land stopped. Your father's rancho becomes mine also, the day we are married, just as mine becomes his."

"The second ambush attempt."

Felicia needed to know all, yet her mind was still reeling with the shock of the Don's words, "marriage canceled—forever."

"Greed knows no bounds. Your life is worth a king's ransom. I was sure who was responsible, so I masqueraded as a bandito... now I have the evidence I needed to keep my relatives at bay. Perhaps peace will come to the Frontier in our time."

"Why... why are you canceling our wedding?" she choked, her anguish almost overcoming her control.

"Felicia," he whispered softly. "Now that the safety of your birthright will be assured by other means, there is no need for a marriage contract between us. I am freeing you to marry whom you wish. Don Warner told me of the lace handkerchief..."

"But I..." She bit her lip to keep the tears back.

"My love, God chose Adam's wife for him and he will choose one for me—a woman as willing as Rebekah. I remembered, almost too late, that even Rebekah's father asked his daughter if it was her pleasure to go with Isaac."

Felicia asked softly, "What did my father say to all that you told him?"

"He seemed relieved. He said that he had learned never to make a contract binding another's heart."

"And are you relieved, Don Andres?" Felicia could barely force her question through her grief of lost love.

"Yes, Felicia, I am. I love you too much to force you..."

She felt his lips touch hers as softly as a whisper.

"And I love you, my darling." Her long lashes fluttered against his cheek. "With or without a contract—I promise you my love, forever."

Her last words were smothered by his mouth covering hers in demanding mastery.

Felicia's heart sang with joy. Love's destiny was hers.